"I Don't Like Your Attitude, Mr. Fortune.

"You're using good old Texas charm to make me feel like a ninny, and then you're going to steal the story out from under me. It's guys like you who keep women down."

"But I like women!"

"Then stop treating me like a bimbo. I want to work. But you're obviously the wrong man to work with, so let's just call it quits right now before—"

"Wait," Nick said, but he couldn't think straight. Just looking down at Lorna Kincaid's beautifully angry face and furious blue eyes was enough to throw him off his usual stride. All of a sudden, Nick found himself actually kissing her right on that pretty pink mouth, but somehow he knew *that* would be a big mistake.

Dear Reader,

Another year is drawing to a close here at Silhouette Desire, and I think it's a wonderful time for me to thank all of you—the readers—for your loyalty to Silhouette Desire throughout the years. Many of you write letters, letters that we try to answer, telling us all about how much you like the Desire books. Believe me, I appreciate all of the kind words, because let's be honest . . . without *you,* there wouldn't be any *us!*

In the upcoming year we have many sexy, exciting stories planned for you. *Man of the Month* is continuing with books by authors such as Diana Palmer, Joan Hohl, Ann Major and Dixie Browning. Ann Major's SOMETHING WILD series is continuing, as is Joan Hohl's BIG BAD WOLFE series. We will have special "months of men," and also duets from authors such as Raye Morgan and Suzanne Simms. And that's just part of the Desire plan for '94!

This month, look for a wonderful *Man of the Month* title from BJ James. It's called *Another Time, Another Place,* and it's a continuation of her stories about the McLachlan brothers. Don't miss it!

So once again, thank you, each and every one of you, the readers, for making Silhouette Desire the great success that it is.

Happy holidays from

Lucia Macro
Senior Editor . . . and the rest of us at Silhouette Desire!

NANCY
MARTIN
FORTUNE'S COOKIE

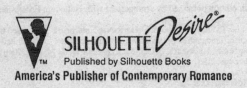

SILHOUETTE *Desire®*

Published by Silhouette Books

America's Publisher of Contemporary Romance

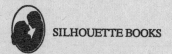 SILHOUETTE BOOKS

ISBN 0-373-05826-8

FORTUNE'S COOKIE

Copyright © 1993 by Nancy Martin

Printed in U.S.A.

NANCY MARTIN

has lived in a succession of small towns in Pennsylvania, though she loves to travel to find locations for romance in larger cities—in this country and abroad. Now she lives with her husband and two daughters in a house they've restored and are constantly tinkering with.

If Nancy's not sitting at her word processor with a stack of records on the stereo, you might find her cavorting with her children, skiing with her husband or relaxing by the pool. She loves writing romance and has also written as Elissa Curry.

One

"She's actually a very good writer," drawled Frank Hoolihan, the managing editor, as he dropped his Stetson on the desk and slurped Scotch from a cracked coffee mug offered by his subordinate. "I've read her stuff. And her name isn't The Dame, it's Lorna Kincaid."

"*Lorna?*" echoed Nick Fortune, setting the bottle on the desk and staring at his boss in disbelief. "Isn't that some kind of cookie?"

"Let me put it this way," Hoolihan said, sliding his bulk into the chair across from Nick to enjoy his drink. "Her last name is Kincaid. Get it? Kincaid."

"Hot damn!" Nick slumped back into his swivel chair and groaned. "Now it's starting to make sense."

"Yes, she's the publisher's niece, and he says she gets a street assignment before she takes over—" Frank affected an Easterner's nasal accent to say, ''—the society column from her aunt, so that's the way it goes.''

Feeling like a punch-drunk cowpoke, Nick shook his head. ''And *I'm* supposed to baby-sit this society girl? Escort her around the mean streets of Dallas and keep her white gloves clean at the same time? C'mon, Hoolihan, what have I done to get kicked out of the bunkhouse like this?''

Hoolihan took another fortifying slug of Scotch and rolled his eyes at the ceiling of the newsroom.

''All right, all right,'' Nick said quickly, sitting up and leaning forward on his cluttered desk, ''so I'm not exactly in the publisher's good graces at the moment— that old East Coast windbag! I admit I did the wrong thing with the Angelino story, but is that one little mistake going to haunt me for the rest of my career?''

''Maybe.''

''But I've been such a good boy lately! All those boring stories out of city hall—have I complained once? How much longer am I going to be punished?''

''The Angelino lawsuit cost the publisher two million dollars, remember—and that's a lot of cattle.''

''But, Hoolihan, I'm the best reporter you've got!'' Nick never hesitated when it came to blowing his own horn. ''Why am I being tied to a kid who probably went to charm school instead of a good journalism—''

''It was a finishing school in Switzerland.''

Nick cursed and sank his head into his hands. He'd been having a run of bad luck lately. ''I can't believe this.''

Hoolihan chuckled. ''Oh, don't take it so hard, pardner. Make things work with J.B.'s niece, Nick, or you'll be pounding the pavement with your résumé in no time.''

"Aw, Frank—"

"In fact, this assignment might do you some good, Nick. If any guy could use a few lessons in charm, it's you."

Nick lifted his head and glowered suspiciously at his boss. "What's that supposed to mean?"

"You're not exactly the domesticated type," Hoolihan said with a benign smile. He'd always been tolerant where Nick was concerned, and the booze made him even more relaxed. "I mean, when was the last time you actually slept in your apartment?"

"The couch in your office is perfectly comfortable—"

"Or had a square meal?"

"Whadaya mean?" Nick demanded, immediately rummaging through the rubble around his computer terminal. "I had a hot dog for dinner—look, here's the wrapper! And a burrito for lunch—see, and the nutritional value is printed right here—"

"Spare me," Hoolihan said, wincing at the sight of fast-food wrappers strewn over the desktop. "Look, Nick, we go back a lot of years. If anybody knows how talented you are, it's me. I'm not forgetting that you got this editor job before I did. But you lost it because you haven't got a management personality. You're a renegade."

"That's not a bad quality for a reporter."

"I know. That's why you're still working here. You're not even forty and you've won more Pulitzers than the rest of these blow-dried types could ever accumulate in two lifetimes." Hoolihan waved dismissively at the roomful of handsome men and women who were diligently hunched over their computers pretending not to hear a word of the conversation between their boss and his rogue reporter. "But," Hoolihan added, "you don't exactly play by the rules, Nick."

"So you think I'm going to learn the rules from a rookie with a silver spoon in her mouth?"

"I'm not looking for miracles," Hoolihan said dryly. "Just try to behave yourself, all right? Lay low for a little while longer—give yourself time."

Nick bristled. "Time for what?"

Hoolihan looked uncomfortable. "Just— You haven't been yourself since the Angelino story fell apart. And if you won't take a vacation—"

"I'm *not* burned-out, dammit!" Nick's involuntary shout raised a few heads around the newsroom, and Hoolihan suddenly looked uneasy. Nick controlled himself and lowered his voice, saying, "There just aren't any good stories that interest me at the moment, Frank. You know how that goes."

Hoolihan nodded, got up and grabbed his hat. "Yeah, I know. And I know you'll pull out of it. You'll be back digging up solid stories in no time. But for a couple of weeks, your job is taking care of Kincaid's niece."

The editor walked like an old rodeo rider—a little bit of a limp along with the bowlegged stroll—leaving Nick to sit sullenly at his desk, glaring at any of the reporters who dared glance his way. Nick fought the urge to punch something, his fists tight on the desktop.

Instead, he poured himself another drink. Then he found an old toothpick in the clutter of his desk, slumped back in his chair and closed his eyes wearily.

An East Coast society writer. Great. Another dull assignment.

* * *

Lorna Kincaid arrived at the *Dallas Bulletin* newsroom promptly at seven the next morning with a spanking-new notebook under her arm and half-a-dozen ballpoint pens ready in her shoulder bag. She believed in being prepared.

She was not prepared for the sight that greeted her eyes, however, when she finally located the desk of Mr. Nicholas Fortune.

The man who lay sprawled and snoring in the swivel chair looked like a derelict who had wandered into the newspaper offices after a week-long drunk, with his socked feet propped on a tornado-ravaged desk tucked into a dim and distant corner of the newsroom.

Never had she expected the great Nick Fortune to look like such a lost cause. She'd read nearly everything he'd ever wrote, cut her journalistic teeth on his work, if the truth be known, and she had always pictured her hero to look something like a cross between Alec Baldwin in a ten-gallon hat and—well, Alec Baldwin.

He didn't look like a prizewinning reporter known all over the country for his hard-hitting news stories and pull-no-punches social commentary. His clothes—a faded flannel shirt worn over a black T-shirt and a pair of ancient blue jeans with actual *holes* at the knees— were rumpled and smelled ever so slightly of stale booze and tobacco. A pair of worn-out cowboy boots lay abandoned on the floor next to a heap of old newspapers that must have numbered in the hundreds.

Lorna felt a surge of disappointment well up inside herself. So much for the gunslinger reporter she had always longed to meet. It looked as if he hadn't shaved in many days, and his black hair desperately needed a cut.

It fell across his forehead from a sharp widow's peak. He even managed to balance a toothpick in the corner of his mouth while sound asleep.

He also wore an earring. Hardly standard cowboy costume.

Lorna pushed her round sunglasses up into her blond hair and stared at this wreck of a man, wondering if her dear uncle, J. B. Kincaid, the last of the old-style, cigar-chomping newspaper tycoons had made a gigantic mistake.

She sighed. "Only one way to find out, I guess."

Conscious that the day-shift reporters were arriving at the surrounding desks, Lorna cleared her throat softly. "Good morning, Mr. Fortune."

No reaction. Nick Fortune gave another gurgling snore and didn't wake or budge.

"Ha-humm," said Lorna, raising her voice only slightly and using one corner of her handbag to nudge Fortune's foot. "Mr. Fortune?"

Still no reaction. An hour ago, Lorna would have doubted it was humanly possible to sleep in such an awkward position, but here was living proof. That is, if Nick Fortune was actually alive. To her, it looked as if a quick death might put him out of his misery.

"My hero," Lorna murmured softly, shaking her head. "Dreams sure die hard."

With a swift jab of her elbow, Lorna shoved Fortune's feet off the desk. He gave one last convulsive snort and woke, struggling to regain his balance, blinking like an ornery badger awakened from a warm winter snooze.

"What?" he blustered, fighting to sit upright in his wobbly chair. "What's going on? And who the hell are you?"

Lorna sat on the corner of his desk and raised one narrow eyebrow while Nick Fortune rubbed his sore neck. "Rough night?" she inquired.

"Rough enough," he growled, eyeing her with resentment and sliding his toothpick to the other side of his mouth.

"You look like you just lost the Alamo all over again."

No grin lightened his expression. In a whiskey-roughened voice, he asked bluntly, "What do you want?"

"First off, I think introductions are in order. I'm Lorna Kincaid."

Nick didn't acknowledge her outstretched hand. "Lola Kincaid?" he repeated. "Am I supposed to know you, honey?"

"My name's not Honey. Or Lola, either. It's Lorna. Surely you knew I was coming."

"Why? Did you send a telegram?"

"No, but your editor was supposed to—" Then Lorna stopped herself. For some reason she suddenly knew Fortune was stonewalling her. She crossed her legs and said succinctly, "I'm going to be working with you for a couple of weeks, Mr. Fortune. You needn't pretend you don't know all about it."

Nick Fortune leaned back in his chair, hands linked behind his head, as if to get a better view of the picture Lorna made sitting on his desk. There was a gleam in the back of his dark eyes—a gleam that quickly vanished, but she'd seen it just the same. "I didn't agree to look after anyone, though I admit you don't look like such a bad assignment."

Some men assumed remarks like that were taken as compliments. But Lorna found the crack demeaning—

a way of keeping her on the defensive. She said, "I wasn't aware you'd been given a choice where I'm concerned."

"Looking after beginners is not in my contract. You can look it up."

Lorna hung on to her temper and managed to say pleasantly, "I'm sure we could find the right loophole in your contract, if we wanted to waste the energy, but why bother? It would just be easier to put up with me for a little while."

"I'm not a baby-sitter."

"Do I look like the kind of woman who needs baby-sitting?"

Nick Fortune's dark eyes were fathomless and velvety—just the kind of eyes a woman might like to gaze into over soft candlelight and a tantalizing bottle of wine. His mouth had a sexy kind of quirk, as he touched the toothpick with one long finger, as if preventing himself from saying something he might regret. Instead, he simply gave Lorna a slow smile. "No, I guess not."

"Good. I assure you, Mr. Fortune, I'm capable of doing just about anything you want me to do."

"That's an intriguing thought."

Lorna gave him an unamused smile. "I'm glad you like it."

"What exactly do you have in mind?"

All business, Lorna said, "Well, I know I'm not in your league, even if you have fallen a bit low lately, but I thought I could be your assistant for a couple of weeks."

"My assistant?" He kept his tone neutral. The somewhat obnoxious mention of his recent career setbacks had struck a nerve. "Well, well, that doesn't sound so bad. But I gotta go to the john right now, cookie. You want to come assist me there?''

"I'm not a cookie—"

"You said you're not a honey, either," he returned, hard as nails, "but that's not how we operate in Texas, sweetheart, so you'd better pick one if you're gonna be so choosy about endearments."

Lorna's first instinct was to apologize and make peace, but she decided a guy like Nick Fortune wouldn't respect her if she gave up now. So she ignored the last exchange and said pleasantly, "I don't think you really need my assistance at the moment. Unless you're more hung over than you look."

He shot her a glower and apparently decided to stop the squabble before he lost control of it. "Just get me a cup of coffee," he growled, getting up from his chair. "I'll be back in a minute."

"I'm no gofer," Lorna said quickly. "I'm not here to bring coffee and Danish while you—"

"Just go get it, Cookie," Nick snapped. He threw his toothpick into the trash can. "Next time, it'll be my turn. Around here, getting coffee's considered a professional courtesy. Lesson one— Lighten up."

He grabbed a toothbrush out of the top desk drawer and departed, striding toward the men's room in his socked feet without looking back.

"That wasn't exactly getting off on the right foot," Lorna muttered. She set her shoulder bag on the desk and wondered if it was possible for a first meeting to go any worse than this one had. Most of it was his fault, of course. But somehow she had managed to completely alienate Nick Fortune and make herself feel like a witch at the same time.

Lighten up. Not bad advice, really.

Lorna knew she'd come to Dallas with a chip on her shoulder. She had a few things to prove—to herself, mainly. But coming on like a tough-minded female version of General MacArthur wasn't her nature. She made an inner vow to calm down and be the old Lorna Kincaid who could work with cocky men without getting uptight. Nick Fortune was smart enough to guess that a lot of bravado was hiding troubles, and Lorna felt it was time to put those troubles behind her.

Spurred on by a few sympathetic looks from the reporters busily working at other desks, Lorna gathered up her pride and set off in search of breakfast for her new colleague. She found coffee and doughnuts on a table by the elevator, poured two disposable cups full and arranged a selection of the least sugary confections on a plate. Balancing the load carefully, she carried everything back to Nick Fortune's lair in the corner.

Maybe he'll come out of the men's room like Superman exiting the phone booth, she thought. He could certainly use a change of clothes. And maybe a change in personality, too.

With that hope in mind, Lorna gingerly dumped fast-food containers into the trash can and cleared a space on the desk as the great Nick Fortune returned. He didn't look much better than he had a few minutes ago.

He grabbed one of the coffees and gulped it hurriedly, no doubt scalding the inside of his mouth. But he didn't seem to notice. Instead, he sized up Lorna over the rim of the cup while the caffeine kicked in.

Lorna did her best to return his gaze in a friendly way. "Well? Are you going to cooperate, or do I need to call for backup?"

He prowled around the desk. "I don't like being forced to look after the boss's daughter."

"I'm his niece," she corrected, prepared to take grief for her relationship to J. B. Kincaid. She'd been doing it all her life—especially since her decision to make a career in journalism despite the cries of nepotism wherever she went. "But you won't need to look after me."

In a mutter, Nick said, "Why the hell couldn't you have picked somebody else to tag along with?"

"Because you're the best," Lorna said, knowing his question was rhetorical, but deciding to answer just the same. "And not just at this paper, but in the whole country—when you want to be. Anyone will tell you that."

"Flattery won't help," he warned.

With a shrug, she said, "It's the truth."

He flung himself into his chair again and slugged more coffee, not arguing with her opinion of his work. "All right, tell me about yourself."

Lorna ventured a smile. "It's a little late for a job interview. I've already been hired, you know."

"Just talk."

Lorna didn't sit on the edge of his desk again, but strolled around his little corner with her chin raised. "What do you want to know?"

"For starters, how old are you?"

"Twenty-nine."

"You look younger."

She decided not to take offense at his tone. "Thanks. How old are you?"

"Thirty-eight."

"You look older."

He shot her another hot glance. "If I want your opinion, Cookie, I'll ask for it. Remember, I'm the old pro and you're the assistant. Now—how long have you been out of school?"

"Nine years. I moved around the country a lot at first, working as an intern in whatever paper my uncle needed help." Lorna decided not to mention her stint in Dallas—and her longing to come upstairs to meet the great Nick Fortune, even then. At that time, she'd been too intimidated to introduce herself to her idol—a fact she'd like to keep from him for the time being. She continued, "I think it was a good way to learn the ropes, doing a little bit of everything. Then I moved to New York two years ago."

"Yeah? How are things on the society pages in New York?"

She narrowed her eyes. "So you *do* know a little something about me?"

He shrugged. "Maybe there was someone in the men's room who knew a few things."

She concealed a smile with a twitch of her lips, glad to see him loosening up and hoping she could do the same. "I see. Well, maybe he also told you that I've been spending some time writing on the life-style pages, but my ambitions lie in a different direction."

"They do, huh?"

"I'd like to try hard news."

"Why?"

"Why?" The question threw Lorna only for a moment. "Because—because it's serious, I guess. Because it's important."

"Some people think wedding announcements are important, too." Fortune's sarcastic tone cut deep as he said, "Every doting mama wants to see her daughter's day of triumph in the papers, you know."

"I know," Lorna said steadily. "And I also know that society pages sell newspapers. They sell *a lot* of newspapers, in fact. But I'm not sure I can spend the rest of my life describing dresses and party decorations. My uncle wants me to do exactly that—maybe even some kind of syndicated column eventually—but I'm not ready to make that commitment. I want to see if I can do the real stuff. Journalists can make a difference."

"You believe that "watchdogs of society" garbage?"

"Yes, I do."

He gave a short laugh. "You can't be serious."

"I'm very serious, Mr. Fortune."

Nick stopped in midslurp, and for a moment he eyed Lorna with a different expression—it was appraising, no longer insulting, and in an instant she felt as if he had probed into parts of her brain she'd never examined herself. "Okay," he said at last. "What are you planning to write about while you're here?"

"I thought," Lorna said blithely, "that we could look into the Angelino story again."

She was pleased to see Fortune spill hot coffee down his hand and stifle a yelp of pain. Amazed, he stared at her. "What did you say?"

"I said I thought the Angelino story needed a second look. I thought—"

"Apparently you didn't think very long," Nick snapped. "The Angelino case cost your uncle a bundle, and he's still royally pissed about the whole thing."

"But the story's not finished yet, is it?"

"As far as this newspaper is concerned, yes."

"What about you, personally?"

Nick frowned and looked away, perhaps to keep his thoughts to himself.

Lorna took the opportunity to study him all over again. There was a quickness of intelligence in his face, a hint of substance beneath the sarcastic exterior. He didn't look angry, she decided. Just weary. Careworn, maybe. With his forehead knitted in a frown, Lorna saw a glimpse of the man she had respected and revered for so long. A journalist with brains and soul.

And he really wasn't bad to look at, either. His body was pretty good, in fact—tall and lean with a certain grace that probably meant he'd roped a few cattle in his day. Maybe he still did. In the bathroom, he had taken a moment to slick his hair back from his face with water, revealing a strong nose, deep-set eyes that seemed to see a great deal, suspicious eyebrows and a mouth that looked—well, damn delicious, once Lorna allowed herself to acknowledge that he might actually be a good-looking guy beneath the disguise.

And it could very well be a disguise. Men sometimes used the slovenly look to keep people—women especially—from getting too close.

He wasn't wearing a wedding ring, either.

Cripes, I never notice that kind of thing, she thought, almost blushing. *How unprofessional.*

He looked back at her and his interest in Lorna sharpened suddenly. His gaze skimmed the pink sweater that enhanced her slim but curving figure. He'd admired her legs before, but now he decided she definitely was not a visiting college coed, but an adult woman worthy of his attention. And he spent a long moment deciding what kind of mind lay behind her earnest face.

At last he set his cup down on the desk and said shortly, "You have any cash on you?"

"Cash?" Lorna frantically tried to guess the new direction of his thoughts. "Yes, sure, I have some money."

"Good," he said, reaching for his boots. "You can take me out for breakfast, Cookie, and tell me everything you know about the Angelino story."

They rode the elevator without speaking, and once on the street Nick turned left and started walking briskly. The Dallas sidewalk was already hot enough to fry bacon, but the Kincaid woman kept up easily and didn't mind the heat—or the silence. They walked six blocks, and she didn't get breathless, although an attractive sheen of perspiration began to shine on her ladylike nose.

Nick's favorite breakfast hangout was Julio's Dixie Diner. It was wonderfully cool inside, and the food was cheap but prepared well enough to suit a large contingent of regulars. Nick took Lorna inside and slid into the rearmost booth—his regular spot.

Lorna slipped uneasily onto the plastic seat across the table from him. She kept her hands off the sticky tabletop and looked at it with the dismayed fascination of a woman who didn't spend much time in greasy spoons.

"Something bothering you?"

"No," she replied gamely, lifting the strap of her bag from her shoulder and placing the purse beside herself on the seat. She whipped a lace handkerchief from inside it and used the white square to dab her shining face. "Do you come here often?"

Nick usually hated spunk, but Lorna Kincaid managed to look spunky and very sexy at the same time. In fact, he found himself wishing she'd chosen to sit on his side of the booth where he could smell the soft hint of her perfume.

She was a lovely young woman—fastidious in the way she dressed and applied her makeup. Her fair hair was smoothly clipped back from her face with a piece of jewelry—some kind of pearl comb, Nick saw—and her lipstick exactly matched the soft pink of her sweater. The look was both ladylike and sensual, he decided. She probably wore lacy lingerie next to her skin and sprayed perfume on her bed sheets just to please herself.

She was the kind of neat, pretty woman a man might like to muss up in bed. Or see walking around wearing his shirt and nothing else after a long, delicious night of lovemaking.

But she was also smart and observant, so Nick quickly brushed those thoughts aside before she figured out where his imagination had gone. "I come here every morning," he said. "Hi, Julio."

The owner of the diner wordlessly approached the table with a thick white mug and a pot of coffee, which he left sitting in front of Nick. He wore a spattered apron with a pack of cigarettes rolled into the sleeve of his T-shirt. He didn't acknowledge Nick—never did, really—and turned to Lorna with a disinterested expression.

When she realized he was asking for her preference in morning beverages, she said, "Do you have any tea? Herbal, perhaps?"

Still not speaking, Julio gave Nick a what's-with-her look.

"She's new in town," Nick explained.

Realizing her *faux pas,* she said hastily, "Any kind of tea will do, then. And—maybe a muffin, please?"

Julio nodded and turned away, leaving them alone in the booth once again. Nick poured himself another cup of coffee. "Okay, kid, start talking."

She sat stiffly, arms at her sides, and didn't take her sharp gaze from his face. "You can call me Cookie, if you must," she said calmly. "But I'm not a kid, Mr. Fortune."

"Yeah, yeah, well, tell me what you know about Martin Angelino, and then we'll see."

"So you might be interested in opening your investigation again?"

He laughed shortly. "Where did you pick up your lingo? Old episodes of 'Lou Grant'?"

"I just want to know if I'm wasting my time with you, Mr. Fortune."

"Wasting *your* time?"

She ignored that and leaned her forearms on the table, suddenly looking serious. "If I give you some new information, would you agree to dig into the story again?"

Nick felt as if a jolt of pure adrenaline had been shot into his system. "What new information?"

She smiled and shook her head. "Let's take this one step at a time, all right? Your last source—the one woman who could have put Martin Angelino behind bars—managed to disappear just before the trial. I want to know if you helped her disappear, Mr. Fortune."

"Where'd you get that idea?"

"It's possible you had a change of heart. Maybe Angelino got to you."

"That's bull! If you knew me, you'd never ask such a thing."

"I do know you. At least, I knew the old Nick Fortune, the journalist. But I need someone reliable now, not a burned-out reporter."

"Are you trying to tell me you have someone who might get the whole ball rolling again? Maybe get Angelino sent to jail for rape or harassment?"

At that moment, Julio returned with a badly burned English muffin for Lorna Kincaid and a full breakfast platter for Nick—eggs drowning in salsa, sizzling hot bacon, a slice of cool cantaloupe and whole wheat toast, the kind of breakfast that always got his attention. But Nick didn't glance at the food. His heart was suddenly pumping hard.

Her steady gaze didn't waver, not even after Julio left. Then, softly, Lorna said, "I know a few things, yes."

"From reliable sources?"

"Do I look reliable?"

"*You* knew Martin Angelino?"

"Well enough to want him rotting in jail as soon as possible, yes."

Two

Lorna was pleased to see Nick Fortune come to attention like a bird dog spotting a fat pheasant in the brambles. He stared at her for a moment, and finally said, "Well, tie me up and brand me with a hot iron."

"I might just do that," Lorna said coolly—much more coolly than she really felt. "But before I grab my lariat, I'd like to help you get the goods on Angelino."

Martin Angelino had been arrested and tried for various transgressions against women, stemming from his improprieties as the owner of a slick apartment building in a fashionable section of Dallas. Several female tenants accused Angelino of harassing them in the corridors and using his passkey to let himself into their apartments without permission. There had been rumors, in fact, that Angelino had lain in wait for several women, hiding in their own bedrooms and forcing himself on them.

Trouble was, none of the victims came forward to accuse Angelino in court, and all of the women who had the courage to bring the lesser charges of harassment against him disappeared before the trial began.

The only guilty verdict against Martin Angelino had come in the *Dallas Bulletin*, under Nick Fortune's by-line. And when Angelino was acquitted for lack of evidence, he sued *The Bulletin* for two million dollars and won.

Lorna was willing to bet that Nick Fortune wasn't ready to give up his crusade against Martin Angelino.

"All right," he said after another moment's consideration of her offer to give him further information. "You've got a deal. Let's go back to the office now, and you can tell me everything. I'll have the story written by noon and—"

"Not so fast."

He stopped, already halfway out of the booth. "What?"

Lorna remained firmly in her seat. "I'm not going to be your source for one article and disappear, Mr. Fortune."

He sat back down and asked suspiciously, "Why not? If you have someone who knows what was going on in Angelino's apartment building—"

"I do, but I'm not going to risk screwing up this story by moving too fast. We're going to play it my way or not at all."

His face turned dark. "Who the hell do you think you are, telling *me* how to write a story?"

"I may be a rookie, but I'm not a fool," Lorna said calmly. "To do this story right, we need more sources than one. I can find those sources, and unlike you, I can get them to talk."

"What do you mean, 'unlike me'?" Nick asked sourly.

Lorna took a breath. "You, Mr. Fortune, are what's politely known as a male chauvinist pig. You're a vanishing breed, I admit, but you and your kind are still happy and healthy and living right here in Dallas. In other words, you're not exactly the kind of person a woman wants to confide her innermost secrets to, if you get my drift."

"I'm damn good at talking to witnesses!"

"At bank robberies, maybe. But when was the last time you spoke to an abused woman?"

Nick looked outraged and bellowed, "All the time!"

"But you haven't gotten the truth out of them," Lorna said firmly. "I've read your stuff, and you can't get into a woman's head, into her heart. It's your one weakness as a writer."

Nick exploded with a string of barnyard expletives that turned a few heads in the diner.

"Don't take my word for it," Lorna said, determined not to give up in the face of his wrath. "Read your own clips. If you have the slightest ability to read your own work with a critical eye, you'll see what I mean. Here. I even have a few examples with me."

"What the hell—"

Nick looked amazed as Lorna pulled a sheaf of yellowed clippings from her handbag. He stared in disbelief as she pushed his breakfast aside and spread the pages out in front of him.

"Go ahead," she said. "Read them."

For an instant, she wasn't sure he would obey. Nick glared at her with the open hostility of a writer who hates like hell to see his work criticized. He looked handsome and angry—a lethal combination. And he also looked as though he'd rather walk on hot coals than critique his own stories. But Lorna pushed the clippings closer, and Nick grabbed them with an irritated exclamation.

While he read, with a rather attractive frown knotting his forehead, Nick also began to eat the scrambled eggs and salsa. As Lorna watched with something akin to horrified fascination, Nick wolfed down his meal—stopping only once to sprinkle Tabasco sauce onto the whole mess.

His hearty appetite caused Lorna to remember she hadn't touched her breakfast. Cautiously, she picked up her charred English muffin and nibbled it between sips of scalding-hot tea. She was hungry, but a few more moments of observing the thoughtful crease between Nick Fortune's eyes made Lorna forget her hunger. She tried not to watch too closely as Nick studied his own work. But he *was* rather attractive under the scruffy exterior. With a decent haircut and a trip to a good menswear shop, he might actually turn into a heartthrob.

Good heavens, she thought, hurriedly banishing that idea from her mind. *I'm here to work, not to get my hormones in an uproar!*

Finally, Nick set the clippings down on the table. For a few heartbeats, he said nothing and ate the last triangle of toast in one large bite.

Lorna sat still while he chewed. "Well?"

He swallowed the toast and looked up, his black eyes delving into hers. "I think you've got guts, Cookie," he said. "But you're wrong about me."

"Now, look," Lorna began, getting hot at once. "I've read all your articles pertaining to the Angelino case, and I think you did a rotten job of getting those women to speak frankly and honestly about—"

"They were under duress."

"It was your job to gain their trust."

"What am I supposed to do? Escort them to the nearest psychotherapist and wait till they're ready to share their life's experiences?"

"If you could put your pigheaded pride aside for one second," Lorna retorted, voice rising, "you could see that you're just like the guy who abused those women. Naturally they weren't going to talk to you. You're a thoughtless oaf!"

"But I'm no rapist!"

"You've got the cocksure attitude when it comes to treating women, though, and that same glint in your eye when you check out a girl's legs. I saw the way you looked at me this morning. Don't bother denying it. Maybe it's not rape, but that kind of behavior is demeaning to some women and downright intimidating to others. It's definitely harassment."

"You're too touchy."

"Am I?"

"A glint in my eye, as you call it, is a far cry from an attack." Nick's jaw was set as he leaned forward on the table. "Don't put me in the same category as that slime Marty Angelino."

"All right. But I can do a better job of talking to those women than you can. I'm sure of that."

"So why don't you write the story yourself?" Nick demanded.

"I— Well, I—" Lorna's certainty faltered, and suddenly she couldn't hold on to the anger that had sustained her so far. "I—"

"Yes?" Nick's eyes gleamed.

"Okay," Lorna said, her pride stung, "I admit I haven't got your writing ability. I'm a long way from your class, in fact. But I think we could work together. I think we could do the story right."

"You seem damn determined to do this," Nick said, watching her face. "Despite my being a world-class pig, you really want to work on this story with me. Why?"

Uncomfortably, Lorna said, "I know what kind of slime Angelino really is."

"That's it?"

"Of course it is," she replied, trying to remain calm.

A wicked smile began to tease the corners of Nick's sensual mouth. "You're sure? There's not another reason why you're devoting your time to this particular story when you could go anywhere J. B. Kincaid owns a newspaper?"

"I don't know what you mean."

Nick pushed the pile of newspaper clippings back across the table to Lorna. "I don't know many reporters who keep clip files in their handbags—unless it's their own clips, that is. Why are you carting around a definitive collection of Nick Fortune's career?"

"It's not definitive. I only—I just—" Then Lorna realized that Nick had correctly guessed her admiration for him. Furious at herself for actually blushing, Lorna couldn't meet Nick's amused gaze.

"Come clean, Cookie." His grin was teasing, but warm. "You may look like the lady who invented Sunday school, but you really want to work with me, don't you?"

"You're a good reporter," Lorna said, still doggedly trying to stay cool. "I'm sure I could learn from you."

"What about the way you were looking at me?"

She frowned. "I beg your pardon?"

"You heard me. I'm not blind. You had yourself a pretty good peek at me when we first met, too. I wasn't the only one getting an eyeful."

"The only thing I see at the moment," she said tartly, "is a monumental ego."

Nick laughed. "Tell the truth, Cookie."

"The truth is that I want to see Martin Angelino pay for what he's done to a lot of women."

He gave up trying to pin her down. "And what exactly has he done? To a nice girl like you, I mean?"

"That's none of your business," she replied. "At least, for now."

"For now?"

"I have no intention of sharing my experience with you, Mr. Fortune."

"Because I'm a pig?"

"Because you wouldn't understand," Lorna said quietly.

"Try me." Nick was suddenly intense. "Tell me what you've got, and we'll go from there. Do you have the story or not?"

"That's what you want, isn't it? Just the story."

"You can bet the ranch on that, Cookie. This kind of reporting doesn't require kid gloves and good manners. It's tough on the streets, and you can't take it— that's clear. So how about you tell me everything and we can move on to the more interesting stuff."

"Which is?" Lorna asked coldly.

He gave her a sexy smile. "You tell me. What'd he do? Pester you with wisecracks? Try to kiss you?"

Lorna gathered up the clippings, folded them neatly and stashed the bunch into her bag. Fishing some cash from her leather wallet, she placed a few bills on the table and prepared to leave—all without meeting Nick's laserlike gaze.

A moment later, she was walking out of the diner with her head high and her heart pounding. She wasn't about to tell anyone—let alone glib Nick Fortune—about her past. She had worked too hard to get beyond it.

"Wait," she heard Nick call from the booth. "Hey, wait a second!"

Lorna didn't look back. She pushed through the swinging door and stepped out into the sweltering heat of the Dallas sidewalk.

She kept walking, but an instant later, Nick burst out of the diner, grabbed her arm and pulled until Lorna was facing him again. His grip was firm, almost intimate. And he was laughing, damn him. "You can't work with me and walk out on me at the same time, Cookie. Make up your mind, will you?"

"Maybe I shouldn't bother."

He released her arm, bafflement dawning on his face. "Why? What'd I do?"

"You don't know? I can't believe it."

"What's going on?"

"You can't take me seriously, can you? You see me as an attractive woman, worthy of being teased for your own enjoyment, but not worthy of working on an important story with, right?"

"I never said that—"

"You said I can't take it on the street. You laugh at me and call me cute names, trying to make me feel inferior. You even call me a 'nice girl' like it's a joke. I don't like your attitude, Mr. Fortune. You're using good ol' Texas-boy charm to make me feel like a ninny, and then you're going to steal the story out from under me.''

"A ninny? I'm only trying to protect you, lady.''

"It's guys like you who keep women down, buster. You don't even recognize it when you're doing it.''

"I *like* women!''

"Then stop treating me like a Playmate of the Month. I want to work and get the Angelino story written. But you're obviously the wrong man to work with, Mr. Fortune, so let's just call it quits right now before—''

"Wait!'' Nick said, holding up one hand to stop the rush of her words.

He couldn't think straight. Just looking down at Lorna Kincaid's beautifully angry face and furious blue eyes was enough to throw him off his usual stride. All of a sudden, Nick found himself thinking about actually kissing her right on that pretty pink mouth—the mouth that was trembling with anger—but somehow in the dark recesses of his mind, he dimly knew that kissing her in that moment would be absolutely the wrong response.

So Nick fought to regain his wits and sputtered "I—I didn't mean to make you feel inferior.''

"I don't feel inferior,'' she retorted. "I said you were *trying* to make me feel inferior. I feel angry.''

"Okay, okay, give me a chance to think straight, will you? It's not every day I have a good-looking woman on my hands who yells at me.''

Her eyes began to blaze even more intensely. "Don't call me good-looking!''

"But you *are* good-looking! Tarnation, woman! Can I help it if you've got my eyes crossed and my—my—'' He tried to come up with an acceptable way to explain how she'd gotten his groin in a knot, but the correct socially acceptable euphemisms didn't readily spring from his brain. All his neural pathways were clogged with testosterone, rendering Nick incapable of speech.

Lorna seemed to guess his drift, anyway, and her expression hardened again.

"Goodbye, Mr. Fortune." She whirled around before he could say more and set off down the sidewalk. Her hair was snatched by a sudden city breeze that kicked up sand and grit from the street and also teased the hem of her already-short skirt, drawing a few glances of admiration from male pedestrians. Nick stared after her in a state of complete confusion. For the first time in his life he stood stock-still while watching a beautiful woman storm away and found himself afraid to say another word for fear of offending her further.

"Aw, hell," he muttered, turning in the opposite direction with a shrug. "Easy come, easy go."

Then he stopped, remembering what Frank Hoolihan had said. "Make things work with J.B.'s niece, Nick, or you'll be pounding the pavement with your résumé in no time."

Nick's first instinct was to forget the whole thing and take his chances. Who needed a touchy female underfoot? Who cared if a good job slipped through his fingers? That's the way life worked. There were other women, other jobs.

Nick had never played by anyone's rules but his own. Maybe he should get into Lorna Kincaid's good graces before he lost his job, but that wasn't the way Nick operated.

He started walking again, but managed to take only two steps before faltering to a halt once more.

Actually, she was more than good-looking, he thought. More than smart. Lorna Kincaid was a woman with a lot of interesting qualities. Soul, for one thing. And Nick liked soulful women. And women of mystery. For some reason, this one in particular really appealed to him, too. He wanted to unravel her mystery, learn her story. In fact, when he considered the matter, he couldn't remember when he'd ever been as poleaxed by a female before. Prickly yet vulnerable, chaste yet sexy—not a bad combination when you thought about it.

He cast a glance over his shoulder, hoping to catch another glimpse of her departing figure. The morning crowd of shoppers had begun, however, and Lorna Kincaid had been swallowed up in the throng. He couldn't see her petite figure anymore or the neat swing of her hips as she walked. He craned his neck and squinted in hopes of catching sight of her blond hair, but she had disappeared completely.

"Damn."

What did he have to lose but his pride? Nick broke into a run, dodging through the crowd to catch up with her again. One pedestrian shouted as he jostled past, but Nick didn't stop. He ran up the street, watching for her, but it was no use. He arrived at the revolving door of the newspaper office and still hadn't found Lorna. Stopping in front of the building he looked up and down the busy sidewalk, but there was no sign of her.

Then Nick snapped his fingers. An inspiration. He stepped off the curb and plunged into the rush of vehicles—taking his life in his hands among Dallas drivers. Ignoring the blare of horns and the curses that flooded out of the nearest taxi, he waved cheerily and darted

across the street. Miraculously, he arrived at the opposite curb unscathed.

Across from the newspaper office lay a small munic-
ipal park—a postage-stamp-size plot of ground with a
handful of trees, some cacti, a few blades of grass and
a pretty fountain that babbled with sparkling water
year-round. It was a minuscule spot of serenity amid the
heat and confusion of the city—a place where Nick had
been known to run to when he needed time alone.

He was willing to bet the park had drawn Lorna Kincaid instinctively.

And he was right.

There she was, her back to him, leaning against a
pillar with her head bent, her face concealed by her lace
hankie. From her posture, Nick immediately guessed
her state of mind, and he felt a pang of regret. He'd
upset her. Made her cry. By acting like a jerk.

There is probably no worse sin for a Texas gentleman to commit than to hurt a lady. Suddenly Nick
heard the stern voice of his own grandfather, saying,
"Boy, don't you ever make a young lady cry. I hear
you've gone and done something hellacious like that,
why, I'll string you up a tree by your heels and hang you
next to a horse thief!"

Nick visibly winced at the sight Lorna made—that of
tender-hearted femininity weeping into her lace. He
edged toward her cautiously.

The park was at least ten degrees cooler than the
nearby sidewalk, and the splash of water somehow
masked the noise of traffic and lent a sweet freshness to
the air. Lorna leaned weakly against a pillar in the shade
of a spindly tree, speechlessly holding the square of
linen to her delicate nose.

Nick hesitated, then steeled himself to do the right thing. Gently, he reached out and placed hands on her shoulders.

"Listen, I'm—" he began.

She gasped and spun around, and Nick immediately saw that Lorna hadn't been crying at all. Both of her blue eyes flew open with surprise, but only one of them was red and teary.

"What the hell are you doing now?" she demanded, stepping back as if he were a mugger.

"I was going to apologize for making you cry, but—"

Indignantly, her back straightened like a ramrod. "I'm not crying, for Pete's sake! I've got a damned cinder in my eye!" She daubed at it with her hankie again and tried to glare at him. "Go back to your—your silly boy's-club newspaper and leave me alone!"

"Look, I—" Words of apology—never easy for Nick in the first place—failed him. She was lovelier than ever, standing among the fragrant trees, all pink and blond and pretty. The only thing that marred her beauty was the increasing redness of her eye. Nick peered at it and said, "Can I help you with that?"

Her eye had filled with tears, and they began to spill down her cheek. But she shook her head proudly. "No, just leave me alone, please. I can handle it."

"Give me that hankie."

"I said I could handle—"

"You can't possibly see a thing." Nick grabbed the handkerchief out of her fingers and stepped closer. "Let me help. It's the least I can do."

"I don't want—"

But Lorna swallowed her words with a queer gulp as he pressed her against the pillar and touched her chin to lift her face to his. Her lower lip gave a small quiver. Nick touched her cheek then and found that his own hand wasn't very steady, either. Standing this close, he could feel the warmth of her small body against his larger frame. He could smell her perfume again—soft and feminine. Her eyes were blue like sapphires—very large and clear, with thick lashes.

In that moment, Nick was tempted to wind his arm around her and pull her snug against him. He could even imagine how a kiss might taste, how her lips might feel beneath his own. He wondered how her tongue might mingle with his, how her slim arms might feel wrapped around his neck.

But the voice of common sense objected in the back of his head. *Just concentrate on the task at hand, old buddy, before you get your face slapped. J. B. Kincaid's niece could be a lot more trouble that she's worth.*

"Look down," he commanded, carefully holding her eyelid and examining her eye for small particles. He tried to put out of his mind how great she felt pressed against him. Her legs were long and lithe, he could feel the surprising tautness of her lean muscles.

Stiffly, she struggled to put an inch of distance between them. "Wait a minute. If this is another of your—"

"Hold still. That's it. Now look up."

She obeyed, then began to relax ever so slightly against him as Nick set about looking for the cinder in her eye. "I want you to know," she said, "that I don't usually walk away from a fight."

"Good."

"But in another minute, I was going to pour hot coffee in your lap."

"I have that effect on a lot of people." Nick used the corner of lace to very gently remove a speck of dust that was clinging to her eyelashes. He refrained from mentioning that his lap felt plenty hot even without coffee.

"Got it?" she asked.

"Almost." Nick pretended to continue his search for the source of her discomfort. With every passing moment, she felt better and better against him, but he managed to say, "Listen, about riling you up the way I did..."

"Somehow, I get the feeling you've riled up a lot of women in your day."

"Hassling women—you've got to understand, it's the way men are."

"Not all men." Was it his imagination, or did she tremble a little?

"Men worth a woman's time," he said.

"I disagree. You don't have to be a Neanderthal to be—well, attractive to women." She shifted her weight, keeping her face obediently tipped up to his. "Did you get it yet?"

"Not quite. Look, I think I'm pretty open-minded. And I'm a fast learner, too. I was just thinking..."

"Yes?"

"Well, maybe we both have something to learn."

She looked him in the eye then, wary and suspicious. "What do you mean?"

"I'm talking about a fair exchange. You help me learn about women on the job, and I'll help you learn the ropes in the newsroom."

A small flicker of hope lightened her face. "You're serious? You want to work on the story with me?"

"I can stand it if you can."

But she wasn't convinced. "I'm not sure," she said slowly.

With care, Nick used the hankie to brush away the tears that had stained her face. It was a very appealing face, he had to admit. His voice turned involuntarily husky. "What aren't you sure about?"

She remained leaning against the pillar, pinned by Nick's body. "You're not what I expected."

"What did you expect, Miss Kincaid?"

"Somebody more ... civilized, I guess."

Although the tears were gone, Nick continued to stroke the planes of her cheek with the lace, slowly, gently. "A good journalist can't be too civilized. In fact, it helps to be a creature of instinct."

Her voice seemed to catch in her throat. "My instincts tell me I should be running right now."

"Running? From the story? Or me?" He left off stroking her cheek and began to caress the slim column of her throat, especially the spot where her pulse beat softly beneath her pale skin.

Unsteadily, Lorna said, "You're not the kind of man who's easy to work with, are you? And you're proud of that."

"To tell the truth, I've always worked alone. A lone wolf, I guess."

Her laugh was breathless. "The wolf part I understand."

"Afraid for your virtue, Miss Kincaid?"

"No, I intend to focus on the job, Mr. Fortune."

"Call me Nick."

"Nick," she said, sounding far from composed as she lingered in his arms.

He began to smile, enjoying the play of conflicting thoughts that crossed her face. As he drew infinitesimally closer, he could see her fighting with a decision—to keep her distance or to melt a little. Maybe she enjoyed the physical contact as much as Nick did. Maybe not. It was hard to tell. His own insides were roiling with excitement.

She said, "If we're really going to work together, maybe we'd better set some ground rules."

"Trust me, I don't handle rules very well." Nick smiled into her eyes.

She was fighting some internal impulse, Nick felt sure, though she managed to say, "But a working relationship should be based on mutual understanding."

"What's to understand? I need you and you need me. We go after the story, and we both get what we want. It's simple."

She put a restraining hand on his chest, and it felt wonderfully intimate. Softly, she said, "We're very different people, Nick."

"So? That's what makes the world go 'round, right?"

"Why do I feel as if you're trying to trick me?"

"You know the old saying," Nick murmured, bending closer to steal a kiss. " 'Tricks are for kids.' But I believe in the direct approach."

Three

———

He looked so wonderfully wicked with those laughing black eyes and the most tempting male mouth Lorna had ever known. She understood intuitively that he wasn't dangerous at all—he was just a man who couldn't help himself. He was enjoying the moment. Even the small diamond earring seemed to wink with dangerous laughter. All Lorna needed to do was close her eyes and lift her own lips a centimeter to meet his.

As that idea built itself into an urge she couldn't resist—an urge she hadn't felt in a very long time—Lorna felt her blood start pulsing hotly in her veins. The heat that suddenly engulfed her didn't come from the blazing hot sun overhead, but from a secret place inside herself. She trembled with its intensity.

She almost stopped him. *Don't do it, don't do it,* cried a voice inside her head.

But Lorna ignored the voice. She heard Nick's small intake of breath and closed her eyes just as his mouth found hers—hot and insistent, yet surprisingly gentle. Half-afraid to be ravaged by a hot-blooded cowboy, she was even more bowled over by the gentle, yet sensual coaxing of Nick's kiss, the subtle way his fingers slid into her hair to hold her against him.

Lorna heard herself sigh. She almost lifted her hand to his face, almost melted her body against the muscled hardness of his frame. His kiss was delicious. It filled her with pleasure and transported her to a place both exciting and soothing.

And then it was over. Nick broke the kiss—reluctantly, perhaps—and stood back to smile languidly at her. "You're a lot of fun, Cookie."

Appalled—with her own behavior as much as his, Lorna said, "Fun?"

He laughed softly. "Sure, that's what makes all sex so good. It's fun."

"Blast you, Fortune! You're still not taking me seriously, are you?"

"I'm taking you more seriously than you know, Cookie."

She tried to fight her way out of his embrace, to wrench free so she could plant a kick on his shin, by Nick neatly put an end to her writhing by pulling her close and subduing her struggles with another kiss.

It wasn't any rougher this time, but came with a bubbling hot surge of sexy sensations. Their mouths coupled, parted, then ground together once more with such complete abandon that Lorna's brain went blank. Unconsciously, she pressed against his chest, longing to feel every inch of his sturdiness against herself. Then Nick's tongue swept a leisurely path across her lower lip—an exploration, an invitation. Lorna responded by meeting his next swipe with her own tongue—all the while cursing her foolish weakness. Her head spun, her body came alive. She could hardly breathe for the barrage of feelings that threatened to overpower her.

But she broke the kiss with one final iota of self-control and stood frozen, staring up at him with her heart pounding crazily in her chest. Here it was at last—the fear. It had been such a long time for Lorna. She had almost forgotten what a great kiss felt like. But she was suddenly afraid. "Don't," she whispered.

"I think we already have," he whispered back. "Under that cool facade, you're a very sexy lady, Cookie."

"Stop this," she said, voice unsteady.

He surprised her by letting go and stepping back—not a full step, but enough space so she could breathe again. He still held on to her hand and his gaze was full of laughter. And something else, perhaps. Something like excitement. He said, "I didn't think you wanted me to stop."

"I—I didn't," Lorna admitted, trying to sustain her balance by pulling away from him completely and placing her hand on the stone pillar behind her. "Not at first, anyway. I'm sorry. I've been—out of circulation for a while, and I'm— Well, I shouldn't have let you go this far, and I'm very sorry. It was unprofessional."

"Says who?"

"I do. Anyone would. It's just— It's not done. At least, not by any self-respecting—"

"I respect myself," said Nick. "And I respect you."

Lorna glowered at him while her heart settled into something close to a normal rhythm again. "Is that supposed to mean you do this all the time? With every woman who comes to work for *The Bulletin?*"

"Nope. Just the ones who look at me with fire in their eyes."

"I never did any such thing!"

He leaned back against the trunk of a tree, smiling. "You excited me from the first moment we met, Cookie. And you reacted the same way, didn't you? So don't throw the blame for this little tryst on me alone, please. You wanted to see what it would be like as much as I did."

"Well," she said, trying to sound brisk, "now that we've got it out of our systems, perhaps we can get to work."

"It's not out of my system," Nick corrected, watching her without moving. "And I'm willing to bet you feel the same."

Lorna felt herself getting hot again. It was too much! Sexual desire for a man she barely knew wasn't the kind of experience Lorna had every day. It certainly hadn't been on her mind when she asked her Uncle J.B. for a chance to come to Dallas to work with Nick Fortune.

"You're blushing," Nick said, looking amused and cocky as hell while she regained her wits. "What in the world are you thinking?"

That you're my hero and I'm dying to kiss you some more in spite of everything, Lorna thought at once. But she quickly suppressed that idea in favor of a tight smile. It would be a mistake to let Nick know how great he looked in those low-slung jeans—the first man to look good to Lorna in a long time. "I'm thinking we should forget this unfortunate incident and get to work."

"Unfortunate?" Nick murmured, shaking his head. "My technique must be slipping."

"Please, Mr. Fortune—"

"I thought we'd progressed to Nick."

Lorna sighed. "Please, Nick. I don't want to spend my time wrestling with you. Can't we get to work on the Angelino story? I know you're just as determined to see that man go to jail as I am."

He smiled. "Look, I've been doing this job for a decade longer than you have, Cookie, and I've got to tell you that I just don't think you're cut out for it. You're a lady, for crying out loud! Being a reporter means getting down-and-dirty. Believe me, I know what I'm talking about."

"I'd like to find out my limitations for myself, if you don't mind. You'd do the same in my position, wouldn't you?"

He considered the question for a long moment, then suddenly launched himself away from the tree and grasped Lorna's elbow. "Take it easy," he soothed when she stifled a cry. "I'm just escorting you to my office."

"Why?"

"To show you a few things."

"Wait," Lorna said, resisting for an instant. "Let me fix my hair. I don't want anybody to think I've been— That we've—"

"Oh, don't worry," Nick said with a laugh, still propelling her out of the park. "Everybody knows already."

"What?"

"Look up," he said, pointing at the surrounding skyscrapers—all with hundreds of windows that looked down upon the small square of grass, trees and flowers. "Half the population of Dallas has seen the whole thing. Fixing your hair isn't going to change their opinions now."

Lorna gaped up at the windows, and she saw dozens of faces smiling down at her from above. She groaned with embarrassment.

"Don't worry," Nick said, chuckling. "In Dallas, we love romance."

"Where are you taking me?"

Nick opened the passenger door of his dilapidated pickup truck and helped the delectable Miss Lorna Kincaid inside.

"You'll find out."

"I thought we were going to your office."

"That's right." He slammed the truck door behind her, then cut around the hood of the truck, keys in hand. When he'd climbed behind the steering wheel, she was still confused.

"But the newspaper building is right around the corner!"

"My office isn't in a building, Cookie. It's out on the street."

Nick put the key into the ignition and fired up the truck's temperamental engine. It stalled once, backfired with a roar that caused Lorna to jump, then it began to chug and spew blue smoke inside the parking garage.

Lorna started to cough. "Are you sure we'll make it as far as the street in this vehicle?"

"No cracks about my wheels, Cookie. This truck has seen me through some tight scrapes. Fasten your seat belt."

"You won't need to tell me twice," she countered, buckling herself into the seat and tightening the belt as far as it would go.

Nick wasn't exactly sure what he wanted to prove to Lorna. All he knew was that she was the loveliest tidbit to cross his path in a long time, and he couldn't imagine her climbing into a gang hideout or walking into a police holding cell to get a story. She wasn't cut out for street reporting. But obviously, she wasn't going to take his word for that.

As he pulled his pickup out of the reserved parking space and started around the circuitous route to the exit, Nick said, "Tell me what you've got against the society page."

"You mean why I don't want to write for it?"

"You said before that you wanted to write something important."

"True," she said, hanging on to the dashboard while the truck careened around the corner. "I'm also rebelling against my family, I guess."

"Uncle J.B.?"

"Not just him," she admitted. "He's been wonderful to me, to tell the truth. If I'd been anyone else, he'd never have given me a chance to prove myself here. He'd just have given me my assignment and told me to take a hike if I didn't like it. For that, I'm grateful. But the rest of them— Well, they're on your side, I'm afraid."

Nick waved to the attendant of the garage and barreled out into the street. He rolled down his window to allow a hot breeze to stir the already-hot air in the truck's small cab. "Who are *they*, exactly? The rest of your family?"

"My mother, mostly." Lorna followed his example and rolled down her window, too. Already, her face had begun to shine from the heat, but she wasn't wilting. Her hair and clothing still managed to look soft and fresh. From her handbag, Lorna took a pair of sunglasses with gold rims. She slipped them on. "Mother thinks I ought to be writing wedding announcements the way she has been all these years."

"Your mother's a journalist?"

"I'm not sure *you'd* call her that. She does weddings, that's it. The rest of the time she's attending philanthropic events. She loves society parties."

"And your father? Is he in the business, too?"

"My father's dead," she admitted, going a little quiet.

"Oh, sorry."

She shook her head. "I'm okay with that. He's been gone since I was a very little girl. He wasn't a journalist, but kind of a dilettante. He had a series of businesses, all of which failed. Uncle J.B. tried to give him a job several times, but my father could never accept charity. He drank too much and—well, he died by his own hand."

Nick glanced across at her, startled. Looking at her pretty face, her spic-and-span clothing, it was hard to imagine that Lorna Kincaid had come from anything but a comfortable and privileged background. Or was it? Something told Nick there was more to the woman than good grooming and good looks.

"After my father died," she said, impossibly cool behind her expensive sunglasses, "Uncle J.B. immediately stepped in to take care of us. He gave my mother a position suited to her abilities, and there was always a job for me after school or during summer vacations. I grew up in a newspaper office, I guess."

"Any brothers or sisters?"

"None. I'm an only child. What about you?"

Accepting the change of subject, Nick said, "Four of each."

She gave an exclamation of laughter and turned sideways in her seat to stare at him. "Four brothers and four sisters? That's nine children!"

"It felt like more than nine," Nick said heavily, "from time to time."

"Good heavens. Where did you grow up?"

"Here in Texas. On a cattle ranch." A poor excuse for a ranch, but there had been cattle, all right, along with endless dust and hard work.

"In Texas?" Her surprise was obvious. "I must say, you don't sound like a native. Sometimes it's really hard to understand the Texan accent, but yours is—well—"

Nick smiled a little. "I worked hard at getting rid of it. I went to school back East where anyone from a place south of the Mason-Dixon was considered an ignorant hillbilly."

"Where did you go to school?"

"Columbia. New York City."

"I know where it is," she said tartly.

At that moment, it was inappropriate to explain how he'd gone to college and grad school on a series of scholarships and the meager wages he'd earned as a stringer for various magazines and newspapers along the way, but Nick almost told her the whole story. He'd scraped and fought his way through school—there was no other way to describe it. It had taken an extra two years to finish college, in fact, because he'd been so broke.

But he had never lost sight of his dream. Sporadic summer jobs like roping cattle, laying bricks and even waiting tables had kept him going—along with the occasional newspaper assignment, but coming up with the tuition every semester had been the hardest work Nick had ever done. He doubted Lorna could understand the hardships he'd endured to get where he was today. She had been born with the silver Kincaid spoon in her mouth, and she couldn't comprehend how Nick's past had molded him into the toughest reporter in Dallas.

Abruptly, she said, "Are you married?"

He laughed. "Not at the moment, no. Disappointed?"

"But were you ever?"

"I'm divorced," he said. "It didn't last long."

"Childhood sweetheart? A beautiful baton twirler from West Texas?"

With a short laugh, Nick said, "Hardly. Trina is an actress in New York. We met in college, married and got divorced a year later. She does commercials, I guess, and some nightclub singing nowadays. We never . . .''

"Yes?"

"It was never meant to work," Nick finished quickly, wondering how he'd managed to be cool about his abbreviated marriage for so long. He had once thought he loved Trina Steinberg intensely, but he eventually decided it had only been mutual and momentary lust, not love, that had brought them together.

To turn the tables on Lorna, Nick said, "What about you? Are you married?"

"I wouldn't have let you kiss me if I were."

Nick cast her a sardonic look. "'Let me kiss you'? I think you were an equal participant in what happened back there, Cookie."

"I'm not married," she said hastily and turned her head, pretending to watch the sun-bleached Dallas scenery.

"Divorced?"

"No, I never went through with it."

Slowing down for a traffic light, Nick said, "What does that mean?"

"I was engaged," she explained, clearly unwilling to say much more. "But we split up before the wedding took place."

"Which one of you got cold feet?"

Looking uncomfortable, she said, "I guess I did. I never felt..."

"Never felt what?"

She was suddenly blushing again. "Nothing. I just— it wasn't right, that's all."

"No sex, huh?"

She wouldn't meet his eye. "That wasn't it."

Laughing, Nick said, "That's okay, Cookie. The sparks don't always fly with the right person, do they?"

"No, they don't," she agreed dryly. Then, changing the subject abruptly, she asked, "When will you tell me where we're going?"

Nick accelerated away from the traffic light, feeling pleased with himself for some reason. "To see some friends of mine."

"Anyone connected with the Angelino case?"

"In a manner of speaking, yes."

"Then you think I may be able to handle this kind of reporting after all?"

"I didn't say that," Nick replied.

He had a plan—one that Lorna wasn't going to like in the least.

In a few minutes, he pulled the truck into a side street. The buildings weren't as tall or imposing as the ones downtown, and there were a few junked cars parked along the broken sidewalk. A half-dozen teenagers hung around the doorway of a liquor store, listening to rap music on a portable CD player. Nick slowed down as he passed the teenagers, but the kids didn't spare a glance for the battered pickup.

"What neighborhood is this?" Lorna asked, breaking the silence between them.

"Let's just say it won't be on the top of your list if you decide to go looking for an apartment."

"But—"

"Don't worry. Nobody's going to carjack this heap. You can sit back and enjoy the view, Cookie."

"I'm not worried," she replied.

He had to give her points for bravery. Not many women ventured into the kinds of neighborhoods Nick found himself frequenting, but Lorna was clearly determined to show that she wasn't afraid.

"Ah, here we go," Nick said. "And look. Some kind soul has saved us a parking space."

He slid the wheezing truck into the space just behind a police car, which had been hastily parked outside a seemingly burned-out church with a tattered flag hanging listlessly from a crooked pole by the front door. Graffiti had been spray-painted on the church walls.

Two punks were sitting on the hood of the patrol car, looking unimpressed by Nick's arrival. Both were smoking cigarettes.

Nick got out of the truck and slammed the door behind himself. "*Buenos días*, gentlemen!"

The two scruffily dressed young men did not acknowledge Nick's jaunty greeting, but stared balefully at him from behind the mirrored lenses of their sunglasses. Nick went around the truck and opened Lorna's door. Like a gallant courtier, he offered his arm and helped her to the sidewalk.

Lorna nervously eyed the men sitting on the cop car. "Where are we, Nick?"

"Among friends, I'm sure. How do you like street reporting so far?"

"Is that what we're doing?"

"Gathering background information, yes. This way."

He escorted her up the steps of the church, which were littered with chunks of broken glass. They stepped carefully through the open doors and into the surprisingly cool air of the nave. The walls were charred, as if damaged by a long-ago fire. Inside, the floor had been swept.

As they entered the eerily empty church, Lorna clung to Nick's arm with more anxiety than she should have displayed, but the rough neighborhood was a far cry from her usual haunts. Still, she was determined to prove herself and at last released her grip.

"Are we looking for anyone in particular?"

"A contact. One of my regulars."

"You have regulars?"

"Sure—guys who are hooked into different sources of information. I admit they're not all pillars of the community, but bankers and doctors aren't usually involved in crime, are they?"

"Depends on the kind of crime."

Nick laughed. "Why, that sounded positively cynical, Cookie. As I see it, part of my job is knowing where to get information. And here's one of my best providers. *Hola,* Rico."

From the gloom of the church emerged a short, bull-like figure of a man. As he came into the light, Lorna saw he was dressed in faded jeans and a dark T-shirt. His long hair was drawn back from his face in a ponytail, emphasizing the cherubic lines of his deeply tanned face. His expression was anything but angelic, however. With thick dark eyebrows drawn down over piercing black eyes and a nose that had been broken at least once, he had the look of a tough customer, all right.

Unconsciously, Lorna stepped back from him.

"Hey, Nick," Rico said, his voice incongruously melodic in comparison to his squat appearance. "What you doing here, man? And who's the lady?"

"Rico, I'd like you to meet my—uh—temporary partner, Lorna Kincaid."

Rico turned his intense dark eyes on Lorna, and she immediately felt as if the man could penetrate her soul with his gaze alone. He made her think of powerful underworld gangsters, complete with a tattoo on both forearms and a menacing kind of serenity that was somehow more threatening than direct hostility. He extended his large and powerful hand to Lorna, who accepted it gingerly. "Nice to meet you, Lorna. You got stuck with Nick for a partner, huh? You have my condolences."

Lorna smiled uneasily. "I'm sure I'll learn a lot."

"He's behaving himself?"

"No, but so far I haven't been forced to use karate."

Rico laughed at that, his face suddenly turning pleasant. "Just remember, hit first and hit hard."

"Words to live by," Nick said wryly.

"At least where you're concerned," Rico observed. "What exactly are you doing in the presence of a lady, Nick?" His gesture at Lorna seemed to indicate her immaculate clothing and perfect posture. "This isn't your style."

"Believe me, it's not by choice exactly."

"You could do worse," Rico commented, glancing again at the prim picture Lorna made in the squalor of the burned-out church. He sized up the way she looked standing beside Nick, too, and gave them both a grin. "How far along is this relationship, may I ask?"

Steamed by his assumption, Lorna said with false sweetness, "Nick isn't going to be buying any condoms soon, if that's what you mean."

Both Rico and Nick laughed, and Nick said to Lorna, "Maybe I should mention that Rico usually goes by his other name—Father Alvarez."

Lorna's surprise must have been obvious, because both men found her expression very amusing. "Father?" she repeated. "You're a priest?"

"The Lord moves in mysterious ways," Rico said, spreading his hands.

"I'm sorry. I didn't mean— You don't look—"

"Rico and I go way back," Nick explained. "And he's given me a tip or two in the last few years. He's hooked into a lot of interesting people. Like the two guys out front," Nick added, looking to Rico for further information. "What's the story?"

Rico didn't seem to mind Lorna's outburst and said easily, "Oh, the usual. Waiting for action, that's all."

"Right outside a church?" Lorna asked. "That's awful."

"This isn't a church," Rico told her. "Not anymore. We're running a kitchen in the back, but no services are held here. The people in the neighborhood have to go up to Saint Anthony's for anything more than a hot meal."

"You run a soup kitchen here?"

"And a day-care center across the street and a women's shelter around the block. It's all part of the job."

Nick said, "It's the women's shelter we want to know about, Rico."

"You're back on the Angelino story again?" Rico grinned. "I knew you wouldn't be able to stay away from it for long."

"Actually, it's Miss Kincaid's story at the moment. I'm just along to ride shotgun. I thought you could tell her your side of things."

Rico turned his attention to Lorna again, studying her solemnly. "You realize I can't jeopardize the safety of the women who are currently in our shelter. And I can't give you the names of anyone who was with us before. That's confidential. The women with us are trying to get their lives back on track after traumatic problems."

"I understand." *Believe me,* Lorna thought. *I understand.* "What's your connection to the Angelino story?"

Rico sighed, shoving his big hands into the pockets of his jeans. "I'm not happy about what happened. It makes me sick, in fact. We have a lot of women who come to us for help. Usually, they stay in the shelter until they feel ready to go out into the world again. We help them find jobs, night classes—anything they feel they need."

"Like apartments?" Lorna guessed.

Rico nodded regretfully. "Yes, I'm sorry to say that we sent quite a few to Harborside Apartments—a building owned by Martin Angelino. At the time, I had no idea what was going on there. Not until Nick came around and told us."

Nick intervened, saying, "A lot of the women in Rico's shelter ended up worse off than they were when they came here. At Harborside, Angelino picked them out right away and started hassling them."

Rico looked angry. "The women who leave this shelter aren't always strong yet. It takes a while to overcome their pasts. If I'd known they were moving into an abusive situation, I'd never have suggested they go to Harborside."

"Tell her about Angelino," Nick suggested.

With a deeper frown, Rico said, "Martin Angelino was a big contributor around this neighborhood. He used to give a lot of money to the church—directly to me, in fact. I thought he was okay. That's why I started sending women to him in the first place. I trusted him."

"Did any of the women who went to Harborside end up coming back here?"

"A few. But we had sent them to a terrible place, so why should they trust us again? Most of the women who became Angelino's victims have disappeared— gone to other cities, other shelters, I guess. I wish I knew what happened to all of them."

As he spoke, Lorna watched Rico's face fill with anguish, and she realized he was a victim of Martin Angelino, too.

"Like Nick," Rico continued, "I've got a personal reason for wanting that man punished."

"Like Nick?" Lorna asked, puzzled.

A shout came from inside the church, preventing Rico from finishing his story. The three of them turned to see who was coming out through the darkness toward them.

"Hey, Washington," Nick said as a tall, lanky man strode swiftly out into the nave of the church. "You look as cheerful as ever."

"Shut up, Fortune. What the hell are you doing in my neighborhood?"

Lorna stood very still as soon as she saw the gun jammed into the man's belt. He was dressed completely in black, including a bandanna that held his kinky hair under control, and the gun shone dully in the dim light of the church. He stopped dead and shoved his glowering face into Nick's.

"Just passing through," Nick said casually, unruffled.

"Who told you what's going down? I'll kill him, dammit. You scum reporters are always—"

"Take it easy, Washington. There's a lady present."

Washington swung on Lorna at once, towering over her and bristling with hostility that soon turned to sarcasm. "What's this? A pink nun?"

"Hello," Lorna said faintly.

"Oh, sorry, honey. Don't you look like cotton candy, though." Washington's slow smile was hardly friendly. "Good enough to eat."

"Uh, thank you."

"What are you doing with a hard-on like Fortune?"

"Knock it off, Washington," Nick said, laughing. "I'm in bad enough with her already. Now she might want to know what's happening here today. Though, if you feel like talking—"

"Take a hike, Fortune," said Washington. "Looks like you could get a few lessons in class from this nice lady. Or maybe—"

The rest of his suggestion was cut off by a popping sound from outside the church. Lorna didn't recognize the noise at first, but it galvanized all three men into action.

Washington grabbed Lorna by her shoulders and shoved her into Nick's arms. Then he took off running—whipping out his gun—in the direction of the pops. *Gunshots,* Lorna realized. Nick seized Lorna, but only for an instant. He pushed her into Father Rico, who instinctively hugged her close and began pulling Lorna deeper into the church. Nick ran off after Washington.

"What's going on?" Lorna cried, fighting for her freedom. "Nick, wait!"

Rico held on tight, a very strong man despite the nature of his profession and short stature. "Hold it," he panted, dragging her into the darkness. "Wait until the shooting stops."

"But Nick! He doesn't have anything to do with this—this—"

On a breathless laugh, Rico said, "He'll make it his business."

More shouts could be heard outside the church, signaling something, and Rico released Lorna after another moment. Together, they headed outside.

Lorna gasped when they hurried upon Washington, lying among the shards of broken glass on the steps. He groaned and cursed as he began climbing to his feet, the gun still miraculously in hand.

"Fortune!" he bellowed. "Stop that!"

Lorna looked down the street and saw Nick in hot pursuit of a young man in gray sweatpants and a loose muscle shirt. They were both flying at top speed. Then Nick launched himself into the air, hit the kid in the hips and knocked him down. They catapulted over the curb and landed in a tangle on the street. An oncoming car screeched to a halt and barely missed them.

Washington cursed some more and began to run toward Nick.

Rico prevented Lorna from giving chase.

On the sidewalk nearest them lay two more young men—both of them angrily yelling as they were pinned to the hot concrete. One of them was bleeding from his shoulder. On top of them were the two men who had been sitting on the hood of the police cruiser just a few minutes earlier. They had their knees jammed into the backs of the men on the sidewalk, and they were wielding handcuffs.

"They're police officers?" Lorna blurted out.

"You came at a bad time," Rico said. "They've had the church staked out for hours."

"Nick!"

Washington had seized the young man Nick had tackled and was dragging him back toward the police cruiser. Nick followed. He was bleeding from his upper arm.

"Oh, my God," Lorna cried, feeling faint. Fortunately, Rico stepped forward to steady her.

Nick plucked at his torn sleeve, more amused than in pain. "I think the police department owes me a new shirt."

Washington slapped handcuffs on the young man in his custody, but he looked far from happy at what had happened. "You're lucky I didn't shoot you myself, Fortune."

"You've been *shot?*" Lorna clutched Rico's hand for support.

Nick shrugged—a mistake, apparently, because he winced. "Minor wound," he said.

Washington clipped the handcuffs around the door handle of the cruiser and swung furiously on Nick.

"I've seen some stupid moves in my time, but this takes the cake, Fortune! What the hell do you think you were doing?"

"You fell over your own feet!" Nick retorted. "What was I supposed to do? Watch a crack dealer escape while you worked on your suntan?"

"Let the professionals do their jobs!" the cop shouted. "Join the Texas Rangers next time you want to be a hero!"

Nick smiled. "You're welcome, Washington."

"Get him out of here!" Washington roared at Lorna. "Before I arrest you both for vagrancy!"

"That's gratitude for you," Nick replied, his eyes alive with devilry. He jerked his head toward the pickup truck. "Come on, Cookie. Do you mind driving?"

Four

In her hotel room that night, Lorna tried to put the sight of Nick's dripping arm out of her head so she could sleep.

But it wasn't easy.

"How do you like street reporting so far?" he'd asked on the way to the nearest emergency room, nonchalant about bleeding on the truck's vinyl seats.

"There's no need to be sarcastic, Nick."

"Who's being sarcastic? It was an honest question."

Driving slowly in the unfamiliar truck, Lorna had said, "Why do I feel like you took me there on purpose? Are you trying to show me that I'm not suited for this kind of job?"

"You think I got myself shot to prove a point?" He laughed at the idea. "Look, reporting can be a tough job—especially my beat. Accidents happen. It's no big deal. But if you can't take it . . ."

Nick hadn't finished the sentence, but he didn't have to.

In her bed that night after hours spent at Nick's side in the emergency room, Lorna tried to sort out her feelings about becoming a real reporter. But instead of contemplating her future, she found herself thinking about Nick.

God, he was exasperating.

And so damnably sexy at the same time.

It felt odd to be thinking about sex for the first time in two years, but it also felt good.

She blew an infuriated sigh and turned over on her stomach, pulling her pillow over her head and trying to put the mental picture of Nick's best lazy-eyed grin out of her mind. And his body! Even before the doctor peeled off his torn, blood-soaked shirt, Lorna had been mesmerized by the lean contour of his frame.

She could imagine tracing the line of his shoulder with her fingertips. She wondered how his golden skin might feel against her lips.

Lorna didn't have to imagine how his kiss might taste. With a deep-felt moan, she remembered how she'd abandoned decorum and let him touch her cheek, coaxing her into lifting her mouth to meet his. His fingers in her hair, his soft murmur of pleasure—it had been too sensual to resist. When his tongue played an erotic game against her lips, she had thrown caution to the wind. Oh, how wonderfully he'd penetrated her pliant mouth then, playing a deliciously erotic game with her own responsive tongue.

She felt her body quicken with the memory. Even flat on her stomach in bed, Lorna sensed her breasts growing heavy with desire. Her nipples hardened at the memory of how Nick's tightly muscled body had felt against her own. Deep in her belly, she felt the warm, syrupy beginnings of feminine arousal.

She groaned. It had been so long since she'd felt anything like desire that Lorna found she almost couldn't breathe. It felt so good. And so terrible.

What had she expected? Mutual respect from her journalistic hero? Had she imagined he might actually admire her writing? That he might want to talk about the First Amendment over a civilized cappuccino? Maybe he'd give her a few reporting pointers and pick up some tips from her, too?

Lorna almost laughed aloud at her own stupidity. In reality, Nick Fortune had decided Lorna was nothing more than a sex object.

And the worst part was that Lorna found herself not minding a bit for the first time in years!

She flounced over on her back and kicked off the bedclothes, hoping to cool down. *Stop it!* she told her overactive imagination.

But images of Nick's gloriously naked body began to assault her mind, and Lorna gave up trying to ignore her fantasies. She imagined Nick's expression as she might strip off her clothes before him in a slow, erotic dance. She dreamed how he might snatch her limp, naked body into his arms and carry her whimpering with desire to his bed. She'd savor his caresses on her silken skin. She'd writhe beneath his plundering kisses of her neck, then cry out when he took her nipples in his mouth and swirl them with his tongue.

His own skin would feel on fire beneath her fingertips. She loved the strong length of his legs, the wonderful curve of muscle in his hips, his back, his shoulders. He'd groan under her merest caressing touch on his chest and taut belly, and when Lorna would close her hand around him to wring a hoarse exclamation of desire from deep in Nick's throat, she'd have him totally in her power.

He'd want to enter her quickly, but Lorna would postpone that pleasure—continuing to explore his body with leisurely sensuality until he was panting with passion. At last, he'd be unable to hold back any longer. Then Nick would be masterful, pressing Lorna into the bed and satisfying himself greedily.

Lorna groaned herself at the moment when her dream teetered on the edge of a shattering climax. But thankfully, the image of a passionate Nick vanished, and she was suddenly alone in her bed again.

She sat up quickly and reached for the pitcher of water on her bed table. Her hands trembled and the pitcher rattled dangerously on the glass, but she managed to pour herself a cool drink. It felt soothing as it slid down her throat, but the water did nothing to cool her fever.

Then the phone rang, and Lorna spilled the remaining water down her nightgown. With a yelp, she answered the phone.

"Cookie?" It was Nick's voice. "Am I interrupting something?"

"Not a thing," Lorna gasped, plucking cold, wet flannel off her hot skin. "Not a thing. What do you want?"

"You sound upset."

"Not about you," she snapped. "I mean—I just—"

"Did I wake you?"

"Yes," said Lorna. "That's it."

"Boy, you Easterners really go to bed early." He was laughing, and the sound was soft and ever so sensual in her ear. "That's a sign of a lousy sex life, you know."

"Let's leave my sex life out of this conversation, okay?"

"Another bad sign," Nick said dolefully. "Won't you even tell me what you're wearing?"

"Why?"

"Why? Cookie, don't you have any imagination?"

"If you only knew," she muttered, suppressing a smile.

"What?"

"Nothing, nothing," Lorna said hastily. "Look, does this phone call have a purpose?"

"Besides giving you a chance to hear my voice once more before you fall asleep? Yeah, I just called to say thanks."

Automatically, Lorna's mind jumped back to the steamy fantasy she had just enjoyed. Had Nick managed to participate telepathically?

"Cookie? You still there?"

"Y—yes."

"About taking me to the hospital and all," he continued amiably. "That was real kindhearted of you."

"Don't mention it," she replied, relieved that he hadn't guessed the truth about her state of mind. Using the corner of her coverlet, she began mopping the water from her nightgown. "How are you feeling?"

"Like a rattlesnake just bit me," he said cheerily, "but I'll recover. A little bed rest is all I need. Any chance you want to help me out with that?"

The man was impossible. "I'll pass, thanks."

He laughed. "Keep it in mind. I think I'll skip going to the newsroom tomorrow and hang around the old corral instead. Doctor's orders, you know. If you get the urge to drop over and join me, though, the address is—"

"Don't worry about entertaining me, Nick. I'll find some other way to pass the time."

"You sure?"

"I can use the day to track down a few contacts for the Angelino story."

"Well, if you're going to do that," he said, sounding a little more serious, "I could tag along and—"

"I'll do these myself, Nick. And don't try following me. You'd stand out a mile in this crowd."

He sounded amused again. "You think so? Exactly how do I stand out, Cookie?"

"That big ego of yours is visible for miles," Lorna replied, feeling saucy. She didn't want to let him know that there was also a magnetic sexual aura around Nick Fortune—one that she seemed surprisingly susceptible to.

"As long as you're sizing things up," he drawled, undaunted, "there are a few other qualities about me you might be interested in measuring. It would only take me ten minutes to get to your hotel, you know. I could hop over and—"

"Good night, Nick."

"You sure? I can tell you're smiling."

"I may be smiling," Lorna replied, "but I'm also sure I don't need a lonesome cowpoke in my hotel room tonight."

"I'll take off my boots," he offered helpfully.

Laughing, Lorna said, "Good night, Nick."

She replaced the receiver and flopped back into the damp bed, grinning at the ceiling.

On Wednesday morning, Nick wasn't exactly greeted by his fellow journalists with shouts of congratulations. But his triumph had not gone completely unnoticed.

"Great story on the crack bust, Mr. Fortune," called one especially annoying young kid who had made no secret that he wanted to become the next Nick Fortune—as if Nick was ready for retirement!

But Nick managed to give the kid a cool smile. "Thanks, Skeeter. Feel free to take it to your next night class."

"Oh, I already did, sir," the kid replied, eagerly pushing his glasses up on his bulbous nose. Even indoors, he always wore a too-large Garth-Brooks-style cowboy hat to keep his unruly red hair under control. "My professor says if it wasn't for your unfortunate tendency for melodrama, it would have been a story worthy of—"

"Yeah, well, tell your lamebrained professor to—"

"'Morning, Nick," Frank Hoolihan interrupted, smiling, before Nick could tell the kid exactly where his pompous teacher could put the article. "Mind stepping into my office for a minute?"

Nick paused at the coffee machine long enough to pour himself a quick cup. Then he strolled in front of Frank's desk, waiting for the accolades to start pouring in.

Frank sat down behind his desk, and his amiable smile of a few minutes ago faded completely. Sounding like a man who'd sat on a branding iron and was still recovering, he said, "You are the dumbest SOB I've ever worked with, Nick. And if J. B. Kincaid wasn't giving you a chance to save your reckless ass, I'd kick you off this newspaper this morning!"

"Why, Frank, you didn't like my crack-bust story?"

"The story was fine," Frank snapped. "But getting yourself shot in the process—"

"I wasn't shot. Not exactly. Well, maybe just a little. Look, the bandage barely shows!" Nick proudly extended his arm to demonstrate that the white bandage was hardly visible beneath the sleeve of his black T-shirt. He hadn't wanted to keep his wound a secret. In fact, Nick had been careful to dig just the right shirt out of his dryer that morning so the bandage wouldn't be completely concealed. A man had to flaunt his own exploits now and then—since nobody else was going to do the job! "The kid was aiming for somebody else," he told Frank, "and the bullet hardly winged my arm. I was running after the guy, see, because the cops—"

"Will you shut up for one damn minute?" Frank's face was very red, and he had to force himself to calm down with a few deep breaths. Finally, he said, "If you get yourself fatally shot, Nick Fortune, I will not give the eulogy at your funeral. Got that? They can plant you in a pine box in a shallow grave and I won't give a damn, because you have courted death for years!"

"Why, Frank," Nick said, sliding comfortably into a chair, "I didn't know you cared."

"I don't, dammit!"

"Then why the lecture?"

"Because you almost got me fired this time, you maniac!"

"What daya mean?"

"Kincaid!" Frank exploded. "He thinks you almost got his niece killed!"

"She wasn't anywhere near the guns," Nick lied smoothly, pulling a toothpick from his pocket. "She was perfectly safe the whole time. Ask her yourself."

"My blood pressure can't stand two confrontations like this in the same day," Frank said sourly.

"Look, I promise she won't get hurt. I'll be extra careful from now on. That is, unless you want somebody else to start baby-sitting her."

Frank glared at Nick. "You'd like that, wouldn't you?"

Nick didn't answer, but chewed thoughtfully on his toothpick. To be honest, he thought he *would* mind if somebody else started chaperoning Lorna Kincaid around Dallas. He'd spent the last forty-eight hours thinking of little else but her slim body and her quick-witted tongue.

And the decidedly softhearted expression in her lovely blue eyes as she'd watched the emergency room team tend to his wounded arm.

With any luck, Nick guessed he might have Lorna Kincaid in his bed before the week was out. That is, if he could get past the secret she was hiding. No, he didn't want any other reporter laying so much as a glance on the woman unless he was around to protect her.

Frank interrupted his thoughts, saying, "Look, I know I shouldn't be looking a gift horse in the mouth. This crack story is the first decent piece of work you've done in months. Do we owe your sudden attention to the job to her?"

"Hell, no!"

"You're sure, huh?"

"Look, Frank, she's a nice girl, but don't start seeing her as my Muse or something."

"Okay, okay, I won't ask again." Frank's thoughtful gaze never left Nick's face, however. "How is it going with her, anyway?"

"Not bad," Nick, said putting his boots on Frank's desk and relaxing in an attempt to keep his opinion of Lorna Kincaid a secret from his perceptive boss. "We're doing some preliminary digging into a story. So far, there's nothing to write about."

"What story?"

"Oh, you know. This and that."

"She helped with the crack bust?"

"Uh, no, not really."

"Then you're working on something at city hall."

"Well, things are pretty quiet over there at the moment. You know, the mayor's gone fishing again."

"Then what," Frank asked bluntly, "are you doing with Miss Kincaid?"

If Nick told his editor they were looking into the Angelino case again, Nick figured he'd be fired. Either that, or Frank would keel over with a combination heart attack and stroke. So he smiled and said merely, "I bet you'd rather be pleasantly surprised with the final results, Frank."

Frank's expression bordered on anxiety. "What does that mean?"

"You don't want to know, old buddy."

"Nick—"

"Just trust me when I say I won't get Miss Kincaid killed. I don't want to see her getting mussed up any more than her uncle does."

"Oh?" Frank's natural curiosity was aroused again and he forgot to be worried. "That's a change of tune. What's going on?"

With a grin, Nick got to his feet. "Nothing I want to tell you about, Frank."

"You son of a gun," Frank said, shaking his head with a mixture of admiration and mental agony. "Just do yourself a favor, okay? Remember who her uncle is."

Nick saluted his boss and went out into the newsroom once again.

His heart did a flip-flop when he saw Lorna perched on his desk across the room, calmly nibbling a muffin and reading the morning newspaper. She had exchanged her usual short skirt for a pair of jeans, and Nick had to admit the change was amazing. How could a woman look equally delectable in dressy shirts and casual blue jeans? Instead of a prim schoolmarm blouse, she'd found herself a cool blue scoop-necked T-shirt, too. Her soft blond hair was pulled up in a sexy topknot that just begged for a man's fingers. Her bangs spilled over her forehead in feminine wisps.

Nick noticed that nearly every male eye in the newsroom was turned her way. Young Skeeter was especially obvious as he stared at Lorna with a slack jaw.

Nick knocked the kid's big hat off his head and snapped, "Get back to work, Skeeter."

When Nick strode to his desk, Lorna looked up from her newspaper. Although she smiled, her eyes were unusually hard. With suspicious calm, she said, "You lied to me, Mr. Fortune."

"What? Me, lie?"

"Yes, you." Ignoring Nick's most winning smile, she set the newspaper on her knee and pointed a perfectly manicured nail at the front-page story she had been studying. "You told me you were going to spend yesterday resting in bed. But you managed to find the time to write this article, didn't you?"

"Now, Cookie—"

"Look, Nick, I have put up with a lot of grief from you, and I haven't even punched you for calling me that stupid name—yet—but I don't think I should have to worry about you flat-out lying."

"It wasn't like that, Cookie, honest. God, in those jeans, you look good enough to—"

She cut him off. "You intentionally encouraged me to stay away from the newsroom yesterday so you could write this piece! Dammit, I was at that drug bust, too! In fact, if it hadn't been for me and the Angelino story, you would never have been at that church when—"

"Shh!" Nick grabbed Lorna by her arm and pulled her off the desk, placing his own body between her and the rest of the reporters in the room. "Do you want to ruin my reputation?"

"What are you talking about?"

"Just keep your voice down." For good measure, Nick added, "Please."

She blinked those big baby blues at him mockingly. "Please? What's going on, Nick?"

"Just—I don't want everybody to think I simply stumbled on a great story, okay?"

"But the Angelino—"

Nick hissed an inhaled breath and threw his tooth-pick away. "Jeez, woman! Do I have to put my own tongue in your mouth to shut you up?" He glanced around warily to see if anyone had overheard their hushed conversation. Everyone seemed mesmerized by Lorna's appearance, but they didn't seem to be listening. Just the same, he wisely, dropped his voice and said to her, "Don't say that name so damn loudly."

"What name?"

"You know what name!" He glowered at her up-turned face, which had turned lightly pink from the mention of his tongue. "We could both get fired if anybody guesses we're working on that story."

"We could *both* get fired?" she asked sweetly.

"Okay, maybe the big boss's precious niece won't get kicked out on the street, but I could certainly end up on the unemployment line by nightfall and what kind of fun would you have without me, Cookie?"

She ignored that. "I'm angry, Nick. You shouldn't have lied. We're supposed to be partners. I thought that meant we did everything together."

He grinned. "Everything?"

In an attempt to appear stern, she squelched the smile that came automatically to her lips, but her eyes glowed. "You know what I mean."

"All right, I'm sorry. I shouldn't have come in to write up the crack bust without you. But it wasn't like that, really."

"You want to explain what it was like?"

Nick glanced around the newsroom again and made his decision. "Let's find someplace private to talk."

"Wait a minute—" She resisted, but not very forcefully.

Nick used one hand to fish a cellophane-wrapped cake out of his desk, then pulled Lorna along between the various desks of his fellow reporters, heading for the freight elevator behind the reference desk.

"Nick, hold on—"

"Relax. I'm not kidnapping you. Not yet, at least." He jammed a finger into the call button of the elevator and said, "You want the truth, you have to hear it on my terms."

"But—"

"Ah, here we go."

The freight elevator was loaded with large cardboard boxes and manned by a skinny young girl by the

name of Charlene, who frowned as soon as she saw
Nick. "Oh, no," she groaned. "Not you!"

"Here, Charlene." Nick tossed her the cake. "Take
a break. I think Skeeter's at the water fountain. See if
he wants to share a Twinkie."

Charlene caught the treat and stepped out of the elevator, still frowning. "I shouldn't be doing this, Mr.
Fortune. I could get in trouble."

"Everybody deserves a coffee break, honey. Especially you. You work too hard. Run along."

Lorna allowed herself to be pulled into the large
freight elevator by Nick's strong grasp. Intellectually,
she knew she was perfectly safe with him, but her heart
suddenly started to go into cardiac arrhythmia at the
thought of being alone with the man. He looked better
than ever this morning. Even the white bandage
wrapped around his upper arm managed to give him the
air of a wounded pirate.

"Nick—"

"Take it easy," he soothed, closing the heavy gate
and sending the elevator upward with the touch of a
button. "You can always push the emergency switch if
I start getting out of hand."

"That's comforting." The elevator surged upward,
sending Lorna's stomach into a tailspin. Or was it
Nick's presence that did that? More calmly than she
felt, Lorna said, "Are you going to tell me about the
crack story?"

Nick touched another button on the control panel,
and the elevator came to a smooth stop—between
floors. Expertly, he flipped a switch to keep them there,
then turned to Lorna, leaning one shoulder against the
wall of the elevator. "Okay, maybe I don't want my

colleagues to know that the whole story was an accident.''

"An accident?"

Nick shrugged. "It was just luck we happened to be there when Washington's men busted those guys. And I probably wouldn't have written the story at all, except . . ."

When he hesitated, Lorna's attention sharpened. "Except what?"

"I just felt like writing the story, I guess. After we talked on the phone, I couldn't sleep." He gave her another glance, and a wicked light danced in his gaze. "So I came into the newsroom and just— Well, the story wrote itself. That hasn't happened in a long time."

"Why did it happen this time?"

"I don't know. Inspiration struck, I guess."

The picture of Nick wandering into the newspaper building late at night after their phone conversation intrigued Lorna. If she'd had anywhere to go that night, she'd have worked off a little sexual tension, too. "You do that often? Come to work when you can't sleep, I mean?"

"Only when I've got a beautiful woman on my mind."

In just a couple of days, Lorna had learned that Nick Fortune was a tricky guy—a man who hardly ever gave a straight answer and could mostly be counted on to get a woman flustered before he was pinned down to the truth. But she really wanted the truth this time and decided to try bluntness. She said, "I've had something on my mind for a while, too."

His grin broadened. "Oh?"

"Something Father Alvarez said."

At once, Nick's expression turned guarded. "What did he say?"

"He told us that he had a personal reason for wanting Martin Angelino punished."

Nodding, Nick said, "Sure. Because he'd sent so many women to live in Angelino's apartment building before he knew what kind of trouble the man was."

"Rico also said *you* had a personal reason, Nick."

For an instant, Nick was very still.

"How about telling me?" Lorna asked. "Since we're partners?"

"Well, now—"

"Don't give me some nonsense. I want to know what's motivated you to keep after a guy like Angelino when Dallas is probably full of stories you could write and get Pulitzer prizes for. Why, Nick?"

Nick strolled to the back of the freight elevator and boosted himself onto the stack of cardboard boxes. "Look, Cookie—"

"Tell me."

He sighed, eyeing her carefully for a long moment and clearly unwilling to tell his secret. "It has nothing to do with you."

"But it would explain a few things. Like why you jumped the gun and wrote the first story before you had all the facts. Or why you refused to defend yourself when Angelino sued the paper for defamation. Or why you've let your career slide since Angelino walked away from the whole mess with a smile on his face."

Nick's expression turned cold. "Now, look—"

"It's true. All of it."

"It's none of your business."

Lorna went to him and planted herself directly in front of Nick. "If we're going to write this story together, I need to know."

"No, you don't."

"Tell me, dammit! What makes you hate Martin Angelino so much?"

"Because he's the son of a bitch who nearly killed my sister."

Five

"Will you tell me the whole story?" Lorna had asked.

That's when Nick suggested they rustle up a late breakfast, after which he gave the elevator back to Charlene, took Lorna back to the parking garage, got his pickup and drove her about an hour away so that they ended up on a long, empty stretch of highway with nothing in sight except two gas stations and a barbecue restaurant called the Ticklish Rib.

The restaurant was empty except for the bartender, an old cowboy in an apron whom Nick referred to as his Uncle Jake. Lorna doubted the elderly man was any relation to Nick, but they seemed to enjoy a certain good-old-boy Texas camaraderie.

Jake wouldn't hear of serving breakfast so late in the day—it was only eleven by Lorna's watch, but he acted as if sunset was due any minute. He brought them each a very cold draft beer and went outside the back of the restaurant to check on his barbecue and spit tobacco juice into the dust. The sweet scent of sauce and smoking mesquite hung tantalizingly in the air.

The beer was surprisingly refreshing after the hot drive. Desperately dry, Lorna drank half a glassful before asking Nick to continue his explanation.

"It's a long story," he said at first.

"We've got the time." She crossed her legs and leaned back on the stool beside his. "Especially since I'm drinking beer before noon. You might have to carry me out of here."

"That sounds like fun." Nick smiled slightly. He sipped his own beer for a minute, elbows planted on the bar. He avoided looking at his reflection in the dusty mirror. "My sister Tish," he said at last. "She's the one just a year younger than me."

"Yes?"

Shaking his head over his sister, Nick said, "She's always been a sweet girl. But reckless. She married a truck driver before she was out of high school and stuck by him for ten years even if he was a little rough with her."

"Rough with her?" Lorna asked carefully.

Nick pulled a face. "It was hard to know exactly what was going on. She looked okay, but I had a feeling things weren't great at home. Anyway, he had a girlfriend in Alabama, and after a while he divorced Tish and married her. Tish was too proud to take his money, so she went to Dallas and started waiting tables to support herself. She told me she was selling real estate, but I don't think she ever made a sale. Anyway, she was awfully broke and ended up taking an apartment at Harborside."

"The rents are cheap there," Lorna said softly, "if you're pretty."

Nick nodded. "Right. It looked like a great place for her—not expensive and close to work. I checked it out with Rico, and it seemed okay. But Angelino started on Tish right away."

"He harassed her?"

"Day and night. It started at the swimming pool. She only went once, but he got interested and made a nuisance of himself. As time went on, he always seemed to be around—the rich-owner-of-the-building-being-nice-to-the-tenants routine, I guess. Tish liked him at first. But he started meeting her in the laundry room, in the hallways—always by chance, it seemed, but Tish felt she had become some kind of target."

Nick's hand tightened on his glass. "Angelino even started to wait up for her to come home from work."

"Did he touch her?"

"Oh, yes." Clearing his throat, Nick said, "She thought maybe he was just a guy trying too hard to be friendly. But it didn't take long for him to get more pushy. Trouble is, I didn't listen."

"She told you about it when it was happening?"

Nodding grimly, Nick said, "Yeah, but I didn't take it seriously. I was working on a tough story at the time and didn't believe Rico could have been wrong about the guy. Tish figured I was her last chance, and when I didn't do anything to help—well, she gave up trying to protect herself."

Lorna reached out and placed her hand warmly on Nick's arm.

He didn't shake off her touch, but went on, saying in a rough voice, "Angelino really put a lot of pressure on her. Finally, she ended up in bed with him. Next morning, she couldn't stand the sight of herself. She got a razor out of her medicine chest and cut her wrists.''

"Oh, Nick.''

His face was very tight with the painful memory, and the muscle under Lorna's hand was tense as a wire. "Angelino found her himself. He had come back for more, I guess, and she was bleeding to death in the shower.'' Bitterly, Nick added, "he had the decency to call an ambulance.''

"The paramedics came in time?''

"Barely.'' Brushing his hair back from his face, Nick said, "Tish was hospitalized for a long time, and she saw a therapist for a long while after that, too. She got her life back, but—well, she'll never be the same.''

It always feels like that at first, she thought.

"I wanted to kill the guy.''

"What about Tish?''

"She didn't care—not about anything. That's the scary part. She came out of the whole experience just a shell. There was nothing inside her for a long time.''

"Where is Tish now?''

"In California. My sister Janine needed a nanny for her kids, so I helped Tish move out there.'' Nick paused, then said, "Janine's a strong woman. I think she'll be the best medicine for Tish now. Obviously, I wasn't much help.''

"Don't blame yourself, Nick.'' Lorna slid her hand down to cover his. "Not like this. It was Angelino's fault from start to finish.''

He sighed, then laughed without amusement. "I guess I do blame myself for what happened afterward. I should have been more observant. I could have been there to help her prosecute the guy, but she didn't have the strength. It seemed cruel to make her go through it all again in a courtroom." The look he sent Lorna was a little frightening—the gleam in his eye had a steel-like quality Lorna had never seen before. He said, "Believe me, revenge is going to be very sweet, Lorna."

She studied his face, trying to decipher her own feelings as well as his.

"Well?" he asked, trying to sound light again. "Has my story changed your opinion?"

"No," she said. "I know this sounds silly, but I wish you hadn't chosen this moment to use my real name for the first time. Not when you're talking about revenge."

"Sorry." He disengaged his hand from hers and reached for his beer again. "I've always had bad timing, I'm afraid."

"That's not what I meant. I don't—" Lorna cursed herself inside and said, "I'm not sure what I meant. I just—well, for the first time I'm starting to think you might have a heart under that cocky smile of yours."

"Did you doubt it?"

"Of course. You've got the come-on artist patter down perfectly—with a certain cowboy flavor. It makes you seem clever, but . . . shallow."

"Ouch."

"Now I think—well, you must love your sister a lot."

He shrugged. "Tish and I were always together. She tagged after me from the time she could walk. But when I went away to school, things kind of fell apart for her."

"No big brother around to take care of her anymore?"

He sighed again. "Yeah, that's it."

"Maybe you're not giving Tish enough credit."

"What?"

"She's a grown-up person now. It wasn't your responsibility to chaperon her through life."

With a curious frown, Nick asked, "What are you saying?"

Lorna chose her words with caution. "That you shouldn't feel as guilty as you do. Maybe if Tish had stood on her own two feet as a kid, she would have been better prepared to handle her two-timing bully of a husband and a sleaze like Angelino. She became a perfect target for abuse."

"If you're trying to cheer me up, you're doing a lousy job." He smiled grimly. "You said yourself it was Angelino's fault."

"It was. Not yours." Lorna reached out and gave Nick's earring a playful tweak. "Don't be one of those guys who wants to run everything—even the lives of the women around you. That's taking the father-protection thing too far. Why don't you take your own advice? Lighten up, Nick."

"Lighten up?" He started to laugh. "*You* say that? Miss J. B. Kincaid's niece herself? Since when did you climb down off your pedestal?"

"I didn't put myself on it," she retorted. "Look, all I'm saying is that I'm sorry for what happened to your sister. It was bad, all right. But it wasn't your doing. It was Tish's problem to fix, and Angelino was the SOB who caused it, not you. And the revenge thing—well, it doesn't sound very healthy for you to be saddling up your white horse with your career and my uncle's bank account at stake, but... I'm ready to help you do it, Nick."

His black eyes caressed her. "You've got your own reasons, haven't you? For getting the goods on Angelino once and for all."

"Yes, I do. I hate the man's guts! But," Lorna added, sure that she trusted Nick—but not enough to tell him her own story yet, "I can't do anything about him at this moment because I just drank a glass of beer on an empty stomach and I'm almost tipsy."

Nick was laughing as he brushed her bangs off her forehead with one finger and peered closely at her face. "Tipsy, huh? Are you trying to get me to buy you lunch, Cookie?"

"Yes, please. Then we're going to slay some dragons, Mr. Fortune."

"You know," Nick said, drawing a thoughtful line down Lorna's cheek, "I liked you from the beginning, Cookie. You've got brains and beauty. And heart. Lots of heart. I like that in a woman."

Lorna had to admit she was feeling no pain at that moment. She found herself relishing Nick's touch, and she leaned closer to him. "What else do you like in a woman?"

His grin was slow and sexy. "Why do you want to know?"

"I'm curious. You come on like gangbusters, but you don't press your advantage, do you?"

"If you mean I don't hang around hallways waiting to pounce on unsuspecting females—"

"You're not like Angelino," she assured him quickly. "At first, I thought—well, any man who teases a woman when she really doesn't want it is just not playing fair. But you never took the next step."

"Kissing you in the park?"

Lorna smiled and felt her pulse start to race. "I'll take half the credit for that."

Nick's mouth looked so delicious, so sexy at that moment. "I liked kissing you, Cookie. You like to play the virtuous maiden, but I think you've got a hot-blooded side, too, haven't you?''

On a muffled laugh, he descended slowly until his mouth hovered just a breath from hers. His dark gaze—alight with passion and a newfound understanding—met Lorna's for a long, tantalizing moment. Then Nick slipped his hand around her neck and pulled her inexorably into a kiss. She closed her eyes to savor every iota of pleasure. Their lips ground together, then parted, and the kiss deepened to a wonderfully warm melding of mind and body.

I'm lost, Lorna thought dimly. It's been so long for me that it feels new again—and wonderful. Wonderful to not be afraid, wonderful to just enjoy.

His fingertips drew gentle patterns on her cheek, her throat, her shoulder. Then Nick's arm slid around her back, and he pulled her against himself. Without breaking the kiss, Lorna slipped off the stool to stand between his knees. She pressed her slender body against his, relishing the strong male contour of his frame and wrapping her arms around his neck. A muted sigh escaped her throat when Nick finally tore his mouth from hers and began to scatter dozens of nibbling kisses along her jawline, her earlobe and the sensitive skin of her neck.

''It's a good thing we're a long way from the nearest motel,'' Nick murmured between kisses.

''Nick, I—''

''Because you've got me so wound up right now that I can only think about taking off your clothes and making long, long love to you, Cookie.''

Lorna smiled as he tugged the neckline of her T-shirt aside and began nuzzling her collarbone. Knowing she could trust him—and certain she could end it if she wanted—gave Lorna a feeling of power and excitement. With his free hand, Nick began tugging her shirt up out of her jeans. Even more exciting was the distinct hammer of his heart, beating against Lorna's breast. She could hear his breath coming in quick bursts, too.

"I want you, too. Oh, Nick." Lorna felt her knees weaken when he slid one hand up under the hem of her shirt. He even pushed aside her bra and cupped her breast with the palm of his hand, making slow, hungry circles meant to drive Lorna out of her mind.

It worked, too. If it hadn't been for Nick's strong arm supporting her, she felt as if she might have melted into a puddle of female flesh at his feet.

Blindly, he found her lips again, and the kisses that had been slowly arousing before were suddenly hot and erotic. Recklessly, Nick's hand roamed beneath her shirt, sending all her nerve endings into an uproar.

Breathlessly, Lorna played her tongue within the heat of Nick's mouth and savored the resulting groan that vibrated in his chest. Although she loved every moment, Lorna knew it was still too soon for her. She braced her hand against his chest—an unmistakable signal to stop.

Nick blew a sigh and leaned back, eyes closed as if he was fighting his own desire back from the brink of no return. Together, they breathed in shallow gasps. At the same time, Lorna felt relief and regret.

At that moment, Jake reappeared in the restaurant, announcing his return by squeaking the screen door first and letting it slam back into place with a loud crack. Then his boots rang out on the wooden floor, but neither Nick nor Lorna bothered to glance in his direction.

They looked deeply into each other's eyes instead, smiling at the message that was clear in both their gazes. *Later,* they said silently. *Later it will be even better.* And Lorna rejoiced that it was true. For the first time in a long while, she truly wanted to be with a man.

Jake stomped closer and started making conversation while he served huge steaming plates of barbecue. Next came little bowls of coleslaw and a basket of corn bread fresh out of the oven. Then Jake poured more beer and brought a pile of napkins.

Lorna looked at the food in dismay and wondered how she was going to manage a single bite. Inside, she was too riled up to think, let alone eat. Jake leaned one elbow on the bar, and the expectant expression on his craggy face meant that he intended to watch them enjoy his food, so there was no turning back.

"This looks great, Jake," Nick said with a slightly false note of heartiness.

"The best sauce recipe in the whole state," Jake said proudly. "Two years to get it right. And I roast my barbecue for exactly five hours on mesquite I cut myself. I'm not one of them fellers who broils good meat for days. You'll see what I mean. There's no better barbecue in the world, miss. You go ahead and try it."

Lorna sat back down on her stool and picked up a rib. She smiled weakly at Jake. "It smells wonderful."

"Go ahead, take a bite."

She did, and the meat was wonderful—sweet, tangy and very, very hot. *Like sex with Nick,* she thought at once. *This is what going to bed with Nick would feel like.*

Suddenly, she was ravenous.

Nick watched Lorna take her first bite of Texas barbecue, and at once her eyes took on a smoky look. As the meat melted in her luscious mouth, he wondered what she was thinking, because the sultry expression that stole onto her features suddenly made Nick weak inside. He wanted to snatch her into his arms and kiss the stuffing out of her. He wanted to sling her off her feet, carry her to the nearest shade tree and make love in the Texas heat.

As she began to eat with an appetite, Nick watched in fascination. The barbecue sauce clinging to her perfect lips made him ache. It dripped off her fingers, and Nick almost leaned over and licked them clean. He watched her little tongue delve into the meat to taste more sauce, and he felt his throat close with desire. The fire in his belly grew too hot to ignore and he groaned softly.

Jake looked at him curiously. "You feelin' all right, son?"

"Yeah, I—I'm fine, Jake."

"Well, eat then! This ain't no picture show! Have some barbecue!"

To get his mind off steamy sex with Lorna, Nick began to eat, too.

While they wolfed down the food, Jake regaled them with tales of his rodeo days and the various kinds of barbecue he'd eaten over the years. Jake could spin a yarn with the best of them, and gradually Lorna became interested in the old-timer's stories. She nibbled corn bread and asked a question or two, while Nick found himself wondering what she'd look like naked, except for a slathering of barbecue sauce.

"You two sure were hungry," Jake noted when he reached to take their plates away. "How about a nice piece of pie to finish off? I got pecan and lemon meringue today."

"I couldn't eat another bite." Lorna sighed. "But it was wonderful, Jake."

The old cowboy beamed with pleasure. "Well, little lady, I'm sure glad you enjoyed it. Maybe you'd appreciate a cup of coffee instead?"

She nodded. "Yes, please."

Nick had a cup, too, and they found themselves smiling at each other over the rims of Jake's thick white mugs.

The coffee had a sobering effect, thank heaven. Lorna began to think she could trust herself to be alone with Nick again. When Jake presented the bill and went off to get Nick his change, Lorna tugged at Nick's sleeve. "Let's go for a ride," she said.

He turned a sexy smile on her. "Where to?"

"I have someone I want you to meet."

Nick had hoped they might adjourn to his apartment or Lorna's hotel room for an afternoon of erotic pleasures, but he managed to keep his disappointment a secret. "Oh? Who?"

"Someone helpful," she replied, leading the way out of The Ticklish Rib and calling her goodbyes and thank-you-so-muchs to Jake.

Old Jake grabbed Nick's arm and held him at the bar for one last moment. Jake said sternly, "You be nice to that little lady, Nickie. She's more class than you've seen in all your life."

"Believe me, I know."

But Jake refused to release Nick yet. "Don't you go hurting her, son," he said severely. "She's got a delicate nature. I can tell."

"I'll try, Jake."

In the pickup again, Lorna gave Nick succinct directions to a seedier neighborhood of Dallas, but she kept very quiet during the drive back into the city. Nick glanced across at her now and then, and he was pleased to see that she was not unhappy. In fact, there was a glow about her that he found hypnotizing.

When she turned to return his gaze, Lorna smiled. "Ready to get to work, Mr. Fortune?"

"Is that what we're doing?"

"Yes. I want you to meet one of the women who used to live in a Harborside apartment."

"One of Angelino's victims?"

"Yes, but don't call her that, okay? In fact, I hope you'll be extra careful to mind your manners."

"Don't you trust me, Cookie?"

She nodded. "Yes, now I do."

"Now?"

"Telling me about your sister—that was an important turning point, Nick. I'm glad you opened up to me."

Nick tightened his hands on the steering wheel. "Did I have to prove myself before I could meet your contact?"

"She's my friend," Lorna said firmly. "And I don't want to subject her to anything or anyone who might remind her of Martin Angelino."

"I passed the test, huh?"

There must have been a note of bitterness in Nick's voice, because Lorna said, "You're a man, Nick. And a very powerful man. These women we're going to see have all had some tough experiences, and they're not all handling it with perfectly good grace. It's understandable that some of them might be afraid of you. Some of them might be angry. Some might even hate you just because you're male."

"I can hardly wait to meet your friends, Cookie."

She smiled. "I think I can trust you to behave yourself."

Nick hoped he could live up to her expectations. But he had been known to act like the proverbial bull in the china shop from time to time. He only hoped he wasn't going to break too many pieces of china today.

The address Lorna gave him turned out to be a large warehouse that had been refurbished. An understated sign on the building read, Women's Free Film Institute.

"This is it?" he asked, parking the truck by the door.

"Yep. Let's go."

The warehouse was guarded by an electronic lock and surveillance system, which alerted the inhabitants to visitors and subjected Lorna and Nick to a long stare from a camera. Then an extremely tall woman came to the door and allowed them to enter. She was dressed in jeans and a T-shirt that read, Sundance Film Festival.

"Hi, Lorna." The woman greeted Lorna with warmth, but cast a suspicious eye on Nick. "Who's this?"

"Nick Fortune, a colleague of mine. Nick, this is Marcy Hendricks."

Marcy's handshake was the bone-crushing variety, but Nick managed to keep a manly expression on his face.

Lorna said, "Peggy is expecting us."

Marcy's eyebrows lifted. "Peggy? Is expecting him?"

Lorna nodded. "It'll be okay. Shall we go in?"

Marcy allowed them to pass, and Lorna led the way confidently into a large, sparsely furnished lobby. Three different hallways began at the lobby, and Lorna chose the one on the left. Nick was surprised by how well she seemed to know the layout. She conducted Nick past a series of office doors, some of them standing open to reveal women hard at work at desks, meeting in small groups or speaking into telephones. Nick estimated that the warehouse probably housed more than a hundred women, all of them apparently hard at work on different film-related projects. He made a mental note to do some research on the Women's Free Film Institute when he got back to the newspaper.

"In here," Lorna said, pausing at a closed door that said, Editing A. She knocked quietly on the door.

"Come in," called a soft voice.

Nick wasn't sure what to expect, but he was soon introduced to a petite young woman with curly blond hair cut in a boyish cap around her face. She had been sitting at a film editing machine, and she stood up and accepted Nick's handshake without a flicker of uncertainty. But Nick couldn't help noticing that her hands trembled.

Her name, he learned, was Peggy O'Donnell.

And her resemblance to his sister Tish was startling.

"Hi," she said to Nick, her smile starting to quiver at the corners once the introductions were past. "Lorna says you want to learn a few things about Martin Angelino."

Nick caught a warning glance from Lorna. "Sure. If you feel you can talk about what happened."

"Are you going to write about me in the paper?"

Nick looked at Lorna for a clue about what he was supposed to say, but she didn't give him any hints. He decided to go for honesty. "We'd like to," he said. "I've talked to other women who've had trouble with Angelino, but none of them have been willing to let me use their stories. It could be tough, you know. Other reporters are surely going to want to talk with you. And the police, too, if things go right.''

"I've stayed away from the police. I can't—I just—''

Lorna intervened. "Nobody wants to go through a trial alone, Peggy. But together, we might be strong enough to handle it.''

"For the moment,'' Nick added, "we just want to talk.''

Peggy sat down on the stool where she had been working just a few minutes earlier. She put her hand on the editing machine and didn't look at Nick. "It was pretty bad, you know. I'm just starting to get my life back on track. My job here—it only lasts until the funding runs out, and then I'll be back at square one.''

"No, you won't,'' Lorna said encouragingly. "You got this job all by yourself and you're really good at it, Peggy. You'll do it again. As long as you keep fighting for yourself, obstacles like Martin Angelino will never get in your way again.''

Peggy smiled. "You talk like my therapy group.''

With an answering smile, Lorna surprised the heck out of Nick by saying, "I have a pretty good therapy group of my own.''

Nick slid onto another stool beside Peggy. "Look, I don't want to force you into something. If I do, there's a good chance you'll back out when I need you most. If you don't feel like sharing your story with the whole world, I understand. But I hope you won't lead me on and then drop me.''

"That's not a threat,'' Lorna added. "He's just being truthful, Peggy.''

The young woman nodded and dropped her head to look at her own hands. Again, her appearance was so like Tish's that Nick had to remind himself that she wasn't his sister, just another woman who'd been through the same ordeal.

"You know," Nick went on quietly, "It's going to be tough. But we'll be on your side during the whole thing, Peggy. Lorna and I are committed to stopping Angelino from doing what he did to you and a lot of other women. We'll stick around if you need us, okay?"

"You want me to press charges?"

Lorna said, "Not alone. I want to gather several victims and do it together. A story in The Bulletin can help enormously."

Peggy gave Nick a long, meditative look and finally nodded. "Okay. I'll help, too."

She spilled her story then, with all the gory details. Peggy had an excellent memory, Nick thought thankfully. She could remember dates and exact conversations, even after an hour of cross-examination. She'd make an ideal courtroom witness. And she didn't get flustered, either, not until she described the night her landlord raped her.

Nick found himself holding her hand while she wept and told him everything.

Afterward, Nick and Lorna walked outside into the Texas twilight, both shaken, yet triumphant.

"What do you think?" Lorna asked when they were alone in his pickup again.

Nick didn't start the truck's engine yet, but sat staring at the street instead. "I think I want to go someplace and take a shower."

Lorna nodded. She fished a tissue out of her bag to fix her makeup, for she had shed a few tears herself during the long afternoon. "I know what you mean. It was pretty intense."

"The guy is slime. Sometimes I want to kill him."

"We can use the paper against him more effectively," she said. Then, suddenly, "Nick, let's go to my hotel."

He looked at Lorna and saw that she was moved and shaken.

But she didn't flinch from his gaze. "I'd like to be with you tonight."

Six

Lorna almost lost her courage when they got to her hotel.

Maybe I'm not ready for this, she thought as the elevator whisked them to the top floor. Beside her, Nick seemed pensive and aloof, suddenly the great journalist she'd come to Dallas to worship close up. Her hero was flesh and bone, and Lorna began to fear she had gone too far. But then she began to worry if she didn't try tonight, she might never let herself be alone with a man again.

As they got off the elevator, Nick held out his hand, palm up. "Key?"

Lorna fumbled for the card key in her bag, then hesitated just before giving it to him.

"What's wrong?" Nick asked. He stopped walking. "Second thoughts?"

Lorna swallowed hard and forced herself to look up at him. "Would you be angry if I had second thoughts at this stage?"

He touched her cheek with one finger. "After what we just listened to? Cookie, if a woman even *hints* that I'm going too far too fast, I'm going to slam on the brakes. It makes me sick to think there are men who treat women like Peggy the way she's been treated."

"Oh, Nick."

He laughed softly. "Oh, Nick? What does that mean?"

On an unsteady breath, she said, "I think it means I want you to make love with me."

"Are you sure?"

"It's complicated, but—yes. Maybe."

"Maybe, huh?"

She laughed a little. "That's the best I can do."

"I'm a gambler. I like the odds."

He took the key from her hand and unlocked the door smoothly. In another moment, they were in the room and Lorna reached for the light switch.

"Don't," Nick said. "I'm in the mood for romance, not bright lights. Leave it."

"But—"

"There's no need to rush things. Let's order room service and watch the sunset."

Lorna almost kissed him. She hadn't guessed that beneath Nick's tough-talking-journalist facade there beat the heart of a true Southern gentleman.

The windows of her room faced full west, and the sun was hanging low on the horizon—bright orange and surrounded by a vivid halo. The fading sunlight cast a warm glow on the furniture of Lorna's spacious suite— the sitting area with sofa and club chairs covered in pastel stripes, the alcove bar with its shelves of sparkling glassware, and the archway that led to the bedroom. It was easy to see the shape of the massive bed with its plump coverlet and pillows that had already been turned down for the night.

"Some place you have here," Nick remarked, coming up behind Lorna and wrapping both arms around her as she stood in the middle of the room.

She leaned against him, thankful that he couldn't guess how hard her heart was beating. It was better for him not to know what a big step this was for her. "I figured a nice suite would be cheaper than getting a short-term apartment."

And short-term apartments held a certain horror for Lorna, too.

"What would you like to eat?" Nick asked, dipping his head to nibble her shoulder. "More ribs?"

Lorna smiled. "We'll never have ribs like Jake's again. No, something light for me. Fruit, maybe. Some fish."

"Very ladylike," Nick commended. "But I insist you share a decadent dessert. Want me to order?"

"Phone's by the bed." Lorna pointed to the bedroom.

"Why don't you have a shower?" Nick suggested. "It'll make you feel better, I'm sure. I'll take care of the food."

Having him in her room still made Lorna feel overwhelmed, even if she had asked him there herself. Lacking the courage to invite Nick to join her in the shower, she escaped to the bathroom and stripped off her clothing alone. A few minutes later, she was standing under the sharp needles of the shower, trying to relax and giving herself the chance to call the whole thing off.

But when she stepped out from behind the glass door, the time for calling things off was past. Nick was leaning against the marble sink with a thick, fluffy towel in his hands. He held it out, eyes closed. "I won't peek," he said. "Promise."

Lorna reached for the offered towel with shaking hands, then enjoyed the way he enfolded her in the luxurious fabric. "You already peeked, didn't you?"

He opened both eyes then and hugged Lorna against himself. "Maybe one glance," he said with a grin. "But the door distorted the view, honest."

Lorna stood still while Nick massaged the towel against her, gradually drying her skin and simultaneously arousing her with each stroke. Somehow, being utterly naked while he was fully dressed felt very sexy to her. Nothing threatening. Oddly safe, in fact. "Nick," she said, "when we were eating ribs today, I thought I'd die if I couldn't have you in my bed tonight."

"And now?"

"I'm a little nervous, I admit." She tried to smile. "It's complicated for me. I had my own experience with Martin Angelino, you know."

"Are you going to tell me about it?"

"Not yet. Maybe never. It wasn't as bad as Peggy's ordeal. And I'm getting over it."

"You told Peggy she'd be okay."

"And I meant it. But . . ."

He grinned. "Are you asking me to be gentle?"

Lorna shook her head, completely sure. "No, just the opposite, I think. You told me once that sex ought to be fun."

"It's the only way. Giggling in bed," Nick murmured, kissing away the glistening droplets from her neck. "It's my favorite sport."

A discreet knock sounded at the door, and Nick gave Lorna a gentle push. "That's supper. I'll take a shower and be out in a minute."

Lorna wrapped herself in a thick white terry-cloth robe provided by the hotel while Nick started stripping off his shirt and reached for his belt buckle. She fled the bathroom before he was completely nude, and found that Nick had turned on some music in the suite and had lit a candle on the coffee table. Her throat tightened. Somehow, she'd managed to find a man who liked to set the stage for romance.

By the time she opened the door of the suite for the room-service waiter, Nick was in the shower and singing a medley of Elvis tunes.

The waiter rolled his cart over to the coffee table upon Lorna's suggestion, and as he set up their meal there, he cocked his head and listened to Nick for a moment. "Not bad," he told Lorna with a smile.

"Not bad at all," she agreed.

She tipped the waiter and began peeking under the lids of the dishes. By the time Nick appeared, wearing only his jeans, his white bandage and a towel draped around his neck, she could only say, "This is the strangest-looking supper I've ever seen."

"You wanted fun," Nick replied, pulling her down onto the sofa with him and dragging the table closer with his foot. "Let's watch the sunset."

The dishes he had ordered were all finger food—strawberries and grapes, shrimp cocktail, some crudités and dip, a selection of small breads and rolls, hot wings with the all-important side dish of celery, and a very large slice of pie that dripped with chocolate, whipped cream and sugarcoated pecans.

Nick cradled Lorna in his arms—half in his lap, half nestled on the sofa beside him, with their legs stretched out and feet comfortably tucked under a cushion to stay warm—and he fed her a grape with his fingers. It was crisp and sweet, and Lorna immediately began to relax as the sunlight slanted farther down the horizon.

They talked and ate. Perhaps intentionally, Nick avoided the topic of Peggy or anything related to the story they were working on. The conversation meandered, covering a wide range of subjects. He confessed his love for jazz clubs and the Dallas Cowboys.

"That's football, right?" Lorna asked, then laughed when he believed the question was serious.

Being writers, they naturally began talking about favorite authors. Lorna loved the writing of Jane Austen and Dorothy Parker as well as that of Stephen King and Larry McMurtry. "I'm not very discriminating," she said. "I like all kinds of books."

Nick eventually told Lorna about his various brothers and sisters, including the youngest brother who had become a hot young stud on an afternoon television soap opera.

"He's the unlikeliest lover you've ever seen," Nick marveled, crunching carrots. "He's twenty-five years old and looks maybe sixteen. And hair! The guy must use more mousse than Vidal Sassoon ever dreamed of!"

Lorna countered with her tale of dating an actor who used more cosmetics than she did and always chose restaurants with mirrors so he could watch himself.

"I can't imagine watching anything but you," Nick said, offering Lorna a juicy strawberry. "You're a beautiful woman, Cookie." He kissed her mouth lightly before allowing her to bite the strawberry.

"Nick," she murmured after she'd swallowed the fruit and found herself stroking his bare chest. "I have a confession to make."

He wolfed down a shrimp and grinned, "Oh, yeah?"

"My favorite writers," she said, "include you."

"Oh, right, the definitive collection of Nick Fortune clips." He laughed indulgently. "Where did you get those, anyway? The research department?"

"No, I collected them myself. Some of them I clipped two years ago when I was working at *The Bulletin*."

He looked properly surprised. "You worked at *The Bulletin*? When? How come I don't remember? There's no way I could forget—"

"I never went upstairs," she admitted. "I was too intimidated."

"Why?"

"Because of you," she insisted. "The great Nick Fortune at the height of his powers! You were like a god to me."

He pulled a grimace. "Well, I've certainly slipped since then, haven't I?"

"Not really. The crack-bust story was really good."

His arm tightened around her, drawing Lorna even closer as their legs entwined. "Okay, as long as it's confession time, I have one, too."

Lorna smiled, puzzled. "What?"

He avoided meeting her eyes and reached for another shrimp, eating it as he spoke. "I wrote that story because of you. I couldn't sleep after we talked on the phone. You had me so keyed up I couldn't think straight. All I wanted was this—to hold you in my arms and let nature take its course. But I couldn't, so I went downtown and wrote.''

''You must have been thinking straight by the time you got to the newsroom.''

''Not really. I did most of that piece on automatic pilot. Thing is, what I had for the first time in months was energy. The fire was back. The passion for my work.'' Nick allowed his black gaze to rest on hers at last. ''Having you around has started the fire again, Lorna.''

''Say that again,'' she whispered.

''That you started the fire?''

''No, my name. Say my name, Nick.'' She lifted her mouth to his, suddenly feeling too intimate to deny herself a kiss any longer. ''Say it.''

''Lorna,'' he murmured, gathering her closer and meeting her lips with his.

She felt she might drown in the lazy pleasure of their kiss and wound her arms around Nick's neck to make it last and last. Her bathrobe began to slip open, and one of her breasts inched out to press tantalizingly against Nick's naked chest. His skin felt warm, and his breath stopped for a moment as they made contact.

He moved his hand inside her robe, slid it down her back and lingered at the curve before cupping her bottom gently, all the while kissing her with languid care. Lorna began to caress Nick's face, his neck, his powerful shoulders.

The sun must have finally given up and descended beneath the horizon, for they were suddenly alone in the candlelight with hearts beating together in a strange, reckless rhythm.

Lorna's fingertips slid their way down Nick's chest to the tight muscle of his belly. There, she rubbed a slow, meaningful circle.

Nick groaned softly and at last tore his lips from her. "Do you know what you're doing to me?"

"I think you're doing the same to me."

His smile was delicious, and his eyes gleamed with barely suppressed desire. "I like you, Lorna Kincaid. You're a fighter and a kind, softhearted woman at the same time."

"And you," she countered, voice trembling, "are a rogue and a very sweet man."

"Let's not publicize the sweet part, okay?"

"If you say so. Nick—" She caught her breath as he found the soft curve of her breast with his thumb. "Oh, Nick."

"Do you trust me?" he asked, matching the quiet pitch of her voice.

Lifting her gaze to his, she said, "Yes."

"I want to make love to you all night."

"Right here?"

He smiled. "It's not a bad place to start."

Lorna could have stopped him. But the time was right. And that time might never come again.

Slowly, Nick bent closer and his mouth took hers again. Lorna moaned softly. He tugged her robe open more fully, and she absorbed the heat radiating from his body. Then Nick filled his hands with the weight of her breasts, caressing the nipples to excited peaks. A rushing wave of aroused desire coursed through Lorna's bloodstream at his touch. He couldn't possibly want her more than she wanted him at that very moment. She felt as if she were melting inside, slowly turning into a pliant, sensual being in his arms.

He edged her right leg with his, and soon followed with a smooth caress along the length of her inner thigh. Sighing, Lorna opened to his touch and shuddered each time his feathery fingertips drew closer to the place that pulsed with desire. All the while, Nick's kiss grew in intensity, his tongue rolling hers with more and more insistence.

Lorna could feel the tension tightening Nick's muscles with every passing heartbeat, and it frightened her a little. He was strong enough to overpower her in an instant. She curled her fingers into his hair to hold him back.

But he was holding himself back, certainly. Lorna could feel him straining to keep his desire in check a little longer, to give her as much time as she needed to match his passion. And suddenly Lorna wanted more. She wanted everything. She wanted to let go, to fly, to burn up in his arms. Breathing raggedly, she guided his head down until Nick turned, lithely pressing her into the cushions and taking one nipple into his hot mouth in a rushing gulp. Lorna gasped and arched against him, chafing her legs on the rough denim of his jeans and relishing the crispness of his chest hairs on her bare belly.

"You're so perfect," he whispered.

"Oh, Nick, I'm losing my head."

"That makes two of us."

"Please," she whispered, winding one leg around his hip to draw him nearer. "Now."

"Now?" he asked on a breathless laugh. "You must be joking. I'm just getting started."

He explored every inch of her body after that, it seemed, teasing Lorna's skin until every nerve ending was alive and raw. His teeth were sharp on her neck, on her shoulders, even on her nipples. His whiskers rasped gently on her curving belly as she arched beneath him. His tongue invented new ways to wring cries from her throat as Lorna abandoned all her inhibitions. A molten fire seethed in her veins. Nick pinned her to the cushions and alternately made Lorna laugh and choke back tears of frustration.

At last, she gave a mighty heave and pushed him off the sofa onto the carpeted floor. He gave a laughing *whuff* as he landed, then allowed Lorna to straddle his frame. As she knelt over him, he peeled her robe completely from her body. His features seemed taut as he drank in her candlelit beauty. He raised his hands to run them lovingly over her skin.

But Lorna trapped him by linking her trembling fingers through his, shaking her head. "No more, Nick. I can't stand it."

"That's the whole point, love."

She clamped her thighs around his hips and gently rocked there. She could feel the hard length of Nick beneath his jeans, but she hesitated to reach for the zipper, watching his black eyes burn. "You're holding back."

All amusement faded from his face. "I don't want to hurt you."

"Am I really in danger?"

"I want you, Lorna. I want you in every way a man can have a woman. If that's danger—"

"I'll risk it," she murmured, reaching to unfasten his jeans.

But Nick was stronger and quickly rolled, pinning Lorna briefly to the carpet before getting to his knees and finally pulling her up. A moment later, he had swung Lorna into his arms and was striding toward the bedroom. Suddenly Lorna's heart and lungs couldn't coordinate. She could scarcely breathe, scarcely think.

Nick eased her down onto the bed, ripping the bedclothes aside with one hurried hand. "Reach into my hip pocket," he commanded, tossing pillows aside. "Get out my wallet."

"Nick—"

"Do it."

Lorna obeyed, hardly able to control her shaking hands. Then Nick snatched the wallet from her, saying, "Now my jeans."

As he fumbled with his wallet, Lorna managed to unfasten his jeans, but Nick was too rushed to wait for her to finish the job. In another moment, he had stripped off all his clothes and climbed onto the bed with her like a hungry panther. "Open this," he ordered. "I'm afraid I'll tear it."

Lorna could have opened the foil package easily, but Nick made the job very hard by suddenly needing to devour her all over again. With rough hands, he parted her knees, and a moment later his mouth hungrily possessed her.

Lorna cried out and dropped the condom, seizing handfuls of the sheet to prevent herself from clawing his shoulders. A tremendous tide of erotic power suddenly swept through her. Nick drove her body to the brink of a wonderful chasm, then moved to take Lorna in one swift thrust.

"Wait," she wept, "I lost it. It's here somewhere—"

"Oh, Lorna!"

"I had it a second ago—"

Laughing and groaning at the same time, they hastily searched the bed and finally came up with the condom. It took only a heartbeat, to slip it into place, and then suddenly Nick was inside her—so hard, so fast that Lorna climaxed at once. From her throat tore sounds so primitive and joyous, and Nick matched her decibel for decibel. He began to thrust in a long, slow rhythm, relishing the spasmodic clenching of her inner muscles.

It couldn't get any better, and yet it did. She lost her head, crying and shouting, rising to meet Nick's strong thrusts until suddenly the whole world was on fire. Faster, harder, deeper. It was hot and wonderful. Two bodies, two souls—suddenly one in a blazing, exquisite moment that hung on the horizon and burst into flame before sinking into a warm and peaceful silence.

They didn't speak afterward—not for a long, long time. Lorna wondered if she might have dozed off with exhaustion with Nick still firmly inside her, still determinedly holding her against himself.

At last, she felt his lips lingering on her temple, and she opened her eyes to smile at him. "Am I still alive?"

"Barely," Nick murmured. "You're a woman like I've never known before, Lorna Kincaid."

"And you," she whispered back, "are the man who's made me well again."

He eased up on one elbow, then tenderly brushed her hair from her eyes. Curiosity twitched his eyebrows together. "I don't understand."

Maybe it was the wrong time. Maybe Lorna should have kept her secret from Nick forever. But at that moment she felt she could trust Nick with anything—even her life. It felt so good to be held by him, to feel his lips against her skin and know he cherished their lovemaking as much as she did.

"You're the first," Lorna explained in a foolish burst of honesty. "The first lover I've had since Martin Angelino raped me."

Nick cursed softly, and suddenly he was wide-awake. "Why didn't you tell me before?"

"I didn't want it to be an issue," she said, touching the backs of her fingers to his cheek. Now that the truth was out, she could not avoid telling Nick everything. "I've spent two years trying to get my life back where it was, and this was the last hurdle for me. I couldn't bear to be with anyone, Nick. Until now. I was afraid if we talked about it, if you knew how big a step this was for me—"

"I would have been easier on you," he snapped. "Lorna, for heaven's sake—"

"But I didn't want you to be easy on me." Lorna held him down, preventing Nick from rolling away from her at that moment. "I wanted it to be wonderful." She managed a smile. "And it was—is."

He hesitated, clearly torn between putting an end to their evening then and there or staying right where he was. "I wish you'd told me."

"Why? So you could tiptoe around the whole issue? Be nice to me because I was a victim? I've had enough of that, believe me, Nick. I've worked hard to get to this point—a lot of tears, a lot of therapy." Lorna tugged him down again, and they made themselves comfortable on the bed. Nick flipped the bedclothes over them to ward off a chill. As he thoughtfully wrapped her in the sheet, Lorna said, "I'm glad it happened this way."

"I can't believe it," he muttered. "I knew you had a grudge against the man, but I never guessed it was as serious as rape."

"It was. I left Dallas as soon as I was released from the hospital. I never even stayed to help the police. I was devastated."

Nick watched Lorna's face, and he could barely control the anger that welled up inside him. He couldn't imagine anyone hurting this lovely woman. She was too ladylike, too sweet, too much her own person. Hardly keeping his voice in check, he said, "Are you going to tell me everything now?"

She shook her head. "No. You don't need to hear the gory details, and I don't want to tell the story again. It happened when I was working at *The Bulletin* and staying at Harborside in a sublet. I never thought anything like that could ever happen to me, but it did. Now I'm ashamed."

"Don't," Nick snapped, rage bubbling just beneath the surface. "It wasn't your fault—"

"I'm not ashamed I was raped," she corrected, sure of herself. "Mind you, that was the most horrible event in my life, but I'm not ashamed by it. No, I wish I had pressed charges then. But I was scared of my own shadow. And I—I needed to help myself, I guess. So I went home, got some counseling, spent time with my family."

Healing, Nick thought. But he didn't say that. Although he'd felt easy in Lorna's presence, suddenly everything had changed. She wasn't the woman he'd thought she was.

"I'm stronger now," she said, drawing a meditative line down Nick's chest. "I'm almost myself again. I'm ready to face the music. Until I met you, I didn't know how far I still had to go, but you helped, Nick. Really, you did."

Nick wasn't sure how he felt about his role in Lorna's recuperation.

Softer, Lorna said, "I wasn't sure I'd ever enjoy sex again. But you made me see the difference between making love and—and—"

For a moment she seemed in danger of losing her composure, so Nick pressed a kiss to her cheek. But Lorna turned her head at the right moment and met his lips with her own. She must have felt him hesitate, however, because she pulled back and regarded him solemnly. "I ruined it, didn't I?"

"No, no," he began quickly.

"I don't want to change things between us, Nick. The chemistry is too good."

It had been good, Nick's inner voice said. *Don't be a fool and spoil things now.*

But he said, "Sometimes chemistry experiments blow up."

"Look," she said more firmly. "This is my problem, not yours."

"The hell it is!" he retorted. "After what we just did—Lorna, sex like that doesn't come down the pike every day. There's something going on between us and I—I just can't forget what you've told me and—dammit," he finished, running a frustrated hand through his damp hair. "I don't know what to think."

"Do you want to leave?" she asked, her voice sounding small.

"No," he said at once, and that much was true. Only an idiot would leave such a beautiful woman in a luxury hotel suite with candles, food and the promise of delicious intimacy ahead. And if the woman was Lorna, a man would have to be dead to ignore her passionate charms.

Still, he felt disoriented. He needed time to think things through.

"Will you spend the night?" she asked, just as softly as before.

Nick jerked his attention to the present and touched her face. "Yes."

"Will you make love with me again in the morning?"

Nick found himself dipping close for another kiss— a real one this time. "I haven't got another condom."

She smiled tremulously. "Is that the only reason?"

"Yes," he murmured, taking her lips.

But he was lying.

Seven

———

He was a rat, all right. A jerk, a toad and a lousy son of a bitch who should have been dragged out onto the street and shot.

But Nick couldn't help the way he felt.

He slipped out of bed around five in the morning and climbed into his jeans. Then he sat for a very long time in the upholstered chair near the window, waiting for the sun to rise and watching Lorna sleep.

She was so damn beautiful. So talented and brave and caring. Not to mention sexy.

If I had any sense, I'd marry her, he thought. I'd marry her and start making babies. Any sane man would.

But Nick wasn't the kind of man Lorna needed in her life. She'd been raped by a brute, and she needed kindness for the rest of her days. And Nick Fortune had never been accused of kindness. He had never been good at giving women what they needed—his own sister was proof of that. No, Lorna needed a man who could take care of her.

And that's not me, he thought. Nobody had ever accused Nick Fortune of being Mr. Nice Guy.

She gave a small sigh in her sleep and shifted without waking—her hand creeping across the pillow, perhaps searching for the right man even if she was unconscious.

You made a mistake, bubba, he told himself. *Here's a lady who's too good for you. Walk away before you make it worse.*

Nick collected the rest of his clothes and went into the bathroom to dress. Before leaving the suite, he'd have to write a note, at least. Only a colossal lamebrain would leave without a note. He thought long and hard about what to say and began to understand why so many men left without saying goodbye. It was too damn hard. He ended up grabbing a piece of the hotel stationery and a used-up pen to scribble only, "See you at the office, Cookie."

Stupid.

Then he left the room, walked over to *The Bulletin* and tried to work on the Angelino story. He soon realized he was crazy to try. The facts just got too jumbled up with feelings. Around nine in the morning, he gave up, went home and took some aspirin to ease the throb in his arm. In his own bed, he slept heavily.

Around six that evening, he woke to the sound of his telephone ringing. Nick panicked and couldn't decide what he would say if the caller turned out to be Lorna. On the sixth ring he figured he'd better at least answer, but when he picked up the receiver, he heard a dial tone.

After that, Nick lay on his back in bed and tried to come up with a way to explain how he felt.

The first step was deciding who that was.

He gave up eventually, and dialed Lorna's hotel. She wasn't in her room, so he left a message. This one was almost as eloquent as his note. He told the operator to tell Lorna that "Nick called."

Then he went out and bought himself a couple of burritos, some beer and a Snickers bar. He ate the food at his desk at *The Bulletin* and made cursory notes on the Angelino story.

"Hey, Mr. Fortune," a voice interrupted around eight o'clock. "What are you doing here so late?"

Nick looked up from his work screen to see skinny Skeeter standing in front of him. "I think it's obvious, Skeeter. I'm keeping the free world safe for democracy. What the hell are you doing here?"

The kid smiled. "Just checking some facts, that's all. That Miss Kincaid was looking for you earlier today."

Nick reached for the long-necked bottle of beer and took a swig. "She was, huh?"

"Yeah, but nobody knew where you were, so she talked to Hoolihan for a while and worked a little bit on your computer."

"Oh, yeah? On what?"

Skeeter shrugged dismissively. "Who knows? Maybe some society stuff. I hear she's a fluff writer."

Nick's temper flared. "She's a hell of a lot more than that, you little twerp. Go home. I hear your baby-sitter calling."

Skeeter looked stricken and made a dash for the door.

Great, Nick thought to himself. *Now you're beating up on kids, too.*

He tried Lorna's hotel again. No answer. He wondered if she was ignoring the phone for a specific reason and decided not to leave a message.

Then curiosity got the best of him, and Nick checked
the computer files for the Angelino story Lorna had
been working on. Within a couple of minutes, he had
her words glowing on his screen. She was a surprisingly
good writer, he was glad to note. Not a rookie. Her lead
was strong—it took Nick only a moment to realize that
she was using an old technique of his—and the rest of
the story was in bits and pieces. Obviously, however,
Lorna had chosen to imitate Nick's style of writing, and
he found himself vaguely pleased and ashamed.

He was almost tempted to start editing her story then
and there, but that wouldn't have been fair. So he
switched back to his own version of the same story and
tried to work. He had to admit Lorna had thought of a
few ideas that hadn't occurred to him yet, so he incor-
porated them into his own piece. He'd square it with her
later, he promised himself.

Around two in the morning, stiff and with his arm
thumping again, Nick gave up working and sat back in
his chair to snooze. He'd think about what to say to
Lorna in the morning.

Lorna found herself trembling as she entered the
newsroom the next morning and saw Nick sound-asleep
at his desk, surrounded by beer bottles, coffee cups and
a dozen aspirin spilled on the desk. A copy of the
morning edition was neatly wrapped and sitting on his
chest as if someone had thrown it at him and the blow
had not awakened him from his stupor.

I wish I'd been the one to throw it, she thought.

She stalked across the newsroom, not caring what Nick's colleagues thought about the scene she was about to make, and she shoved his boots off the desk.

Nick woke with a snort and blinked at her blearily.

"Remember this face?" Lorna asked, standing over him with her fists cocked on her hips. "The one you went to sleep with a couple of nights back?"

"Lorna," he croaked.

She feigned amazement. "You *do* remember!"

"Don't be sarcastic. I have a splitting headache."

"Good." She cleared a space in the rubble on his desk and sat, crossing her legs. "Would the pain be too excruciating if I asked where the hell you've been since we made love?"

He looked up from cradling his head in his hands. "You want everybody in the building to know what happened?"

"That you ran out on me after the best sex either of us has had in our whole lives?" Shaking with anger, she snapped, "Sure, but that won't be news to anybody here, will it? They already know what kind of a sneaky—"

He held up one hand to stop her tirade. "Take it easy, all right? It wasn't like that."

"Oh?" she asked archly, barely holding back the tears of anger and distress that threatened to spill at any moment. "Exactly what *was* it like?"

"Lorna—"

"I liked it better when you called me Cookie. At least I knew where I stood with you then."

He sighed and glowered at her. "I tried to call you. I left at least one message at your hotel."

"But you've been ducking me, Nick."

"I don't work in the daylight hours! Ask anybody."

"I'm asking you," Lorna said, steeling herself to hear his answer. "Have you been ducking me?"

"Maybe," he replied, then brushing his hair back from his forehead, he admitted, "Probably."

"Why?" Lorna asked softly. "What did I do?"

"Nothing. It's not you. It's me."

Lorna watched him for a long moment, wishing she knew how to get him to talk. "I thought something special happened between us. Something wonderful."

"It did," he agreed, meeting her eyes at last, but looking far from his devilish self. "I'm just the wrong guy for you, Lorna."

Her throat closed with emotion, but Lorna was damned if she'd cry now. Not after everything else that had happened to her. She attempted to sound cool. "It's nice to know you have weaknesses, I guess."

Nick shook his head. "I never claimed to be anyone's hero. I can't be the man you need, Lorna. I'm basically a jerk. You need somebody who can take care of you—"

"I can take care of myself, damn you."

"You know what I mean."

"No, I don't!" she snapped, barely hanging on to her composure. "I thought we established that you can't be a white knight for every woman in your life. Give me a little credit! I'm not asking you to hold my hand and spoon-feed me a lot of stupid sympathy!"

"What in hell do you want from me, then?"

"I'm not asking for the moon. I want some fun! I want to laugh with you—"

"I don't feel like laughing."

"Damn you! Who's the injured party here?"

"I can't help it! I know I'm being a jerk, but I—"

"Children," a voice rang out behind them. "Children, children, let's not turn my newsroom into a kindergarten class, okay?"

"'Morning, Frank," Nick said as the managing editor approached his desk.

Lorna did not turn around, but sat up straight and struggled to control herself.

Frank Hoolihan pulled up a chair and sat down. "Mind telling me what's going on here?"

"A spat," Nick said.

Frank lifted his eyebrows. "Not a lover's quarrel, I hope?"

Lorna said, "Nothing of the kind, Mr. Hoolihan. Nick and I were just discussing our story. We can't agree, so we're going to go our separate ways."

"Wait a minute," Nick started.

"What story is that?" Hoolihan asked innocently.

"Just—"

"The Angelino story," Lorna replied succinctly, knowing full well Frank had forbidden Nick to ever work on the case again.

Nick sighed and sank down in his chair, the picture of dejection.

Frank did not explode right away. But his face turned three shades of purple. Then, sounding reasonably calm, he said, "I thought we reached an agreement on that story a long time ago, Nick."

"Actually, it's my story now," Lorna said.

"The hell it is," Nick growled.

Facing the editor, Lorna said, "I came to Dallas to do this story, Mr. Hoolihan. I should have told you, but considering what happened before, I thought it would be best if I didn't get anyone into trouble with my uncle."

"Do you have his permission?" Frank asked. "If the paper's going to get sued again—"

"I don't believe we have to worry about that," Lorna said. "Not this time. I spent last night with the police, and they're going to go ahead and press charges."

Nick sat up. "You did *what* last night?"

"Peggy and I went together," Lorna told him. "I called your pal Washington, and he agreed to help even if this case isn't his usual territory."

"Washington?" Frank echoed. "That narcotics cop who hates your guts, Nick?"

"The very one," Nick agreed, looking depressed.

Lorna said, "The police think they've got a strong case already, and they're looking for more women to help. They're going to spend today and probably tomorrow talking to women who live at Harborside right now, and they hope to arrest him the day after." Pleased, she noted Nick looked flabbergasted. "But the police think they can get a conviction this time even if nobody else steps forward. They're calling Angelino a serial rapist, and Peggy's going to testify in court."

"What about you?" Nick asked.

Frank sat up suddenly. "What *about* you, Miss Kincaid? Are you involved in this mess?"

"I'm writing the story," Lorna told him, deciding Frank didn't need to know the extent of her involvement yet. Conflict of interest was a serious charge, and she hadn't yet worked out how to avoid it. "I think it would be best if Mr. Fortune went back to whatever stories he was working on before I came."

"Just a damn minute!" Nick began. "That story was mine from the start, Frank—"

"And you got us little more than a lawsuit," Frank finished, raising his voice to match Nick's. "Let's let Miss Kincaid try."

Nick was on his feet by then. "She's not ready for this kind of story, Frank! Ask her, and she'll tell you. She's never written anything but—"

"All right, all right, what do you suggest?"

Nick was breathing hard, and he began to pace around his desk. "Let us both try. Whoever writes the best story gets the byline."

Lorna decided she'd better fight for herself and said, "That's a waste of manpower, Mr. Hoolihan. I've got all the information. Why use Nick for this when he could be writing something else?"

"Because he hasn't got anything else," Frank guessed. "Am I right, Nick?"

Nick spread his hands and smiled. "I've got absolutely nothing, Frank."

"But—"

"I'm through listening to arguments," Frank declared, standing up. "I've got work to do. Here's the deal. Both of you write your story. By four o'clock, I want both versions on my desk. Got that?"

Lorna agreed at once, and Nick looked angry for a moment. "Okay," he said at last, shooting a glare at Lorna that soon melted into a crafty grin. "May the best man win."

Lorna turned her back on him and stalked to the nearest empty desk. *May the best man win, huh?* She dropped her bag on the floor, thumbed the button on the computer terminal and sat down, seething with anger. Within a minute, she was looking at her story and frowning to concentrate and drain all thoughts of the man out of her mind. There had to be a way to make her version better than Nick's.

She shot a cautious glance across the room and saw Nick gulping coffee and glaring intently at his own screen. He didn't look any more capable of concentration than she felt. But then he hunched forward and began to type.

A race to the finish, she thought. May the best man win? How about a woman this time?

She got down to work and feverishly banged on the keyboard for a solid hour. It was good, she knew, but far too long. Without looking up again, she read her first draft and began trimming excess lines. After a cut-throat revision, the story still came out too long, so she dived in again and tried to cut more. But she felt as if she were drowning in words. No matter how she tried, she couldn't tell her story in fewer lines. Struggling with the words as well as her own feelings that kept crowding into the story, Lorna worked and worked without paying any attention to the time.

"Ahem," Nick said, suddenly appearing at her desk.

Lorna glanced up, surprised and wondering how long he'd been standing there. "Yes?"

He didn't smile, but held on to an armful of papers. "Let's not turn on each other like a couple of wild dogs."

"Don't try to be nice to me now, Nick!"

"Dammit, Lorna—"

"I'm sorry. I'm a little tense."

"Me, too. Look, I don't know how much trouble you're having, but I can't write this story without talking to the police. Trouble is, they won't talk to me."

"That's because Peggy and I asked them to keep a lid on everything until after the arrest."

"Lorna, that's not fair."

She skewered him with a look. "You want to talk about fairness?"

"Okay, I deserved that." Nick pulled up a chair and sat in it, scooting closer to keep their conversation private and still hugging his papers to his chest. "I think we ought to try working together."

"I don't need you, Nick."

"Oh, no? Then how come you've been glaring at your screen for the last hour like you wanted to punch the thing?"

"Maybe I was thinking of you."

He allowed a half smile. "Come on, you came here to pick my brains, right? I don't see why we can't put our personal relationship aside long enough to write this story the way it should be written."

"Do we have a personal relationship?"

"Lorna—"

"Okay, okay," she agreed quickly. "It's almost four o'clock. Let's work together."

"Great!" Nick immediately spread a heap of papers out on her desk and offered her an apple, which he conjured from the pile. "Here, hungry?"

"Starved." Lorna accepted the apple and watched while Nick pawed through his drafts.

"I think we ought to use my lead," he began. "It's stronger and—"

"You haven't even read my lead."

"Yes, I did." He had the grace to look a little embarrassed. "Before you came in this morning. It's not bad, but—"

"You were snooping in my files?"

He looked at her hotly. "Are we going to get some work done, or are you going to nitpick everything I do?"

"A little of both," Lorna said gruffly, taking a gigantic bite of apple. "Let me see your lead."

He handed it over. "While you look at that, let me read what you've written so far."

She scooted her chair back, allowing him access to her keyboard. While getting into place, Nick bumped Lorna's knee with his. Instead of jerking back as if terrified of touching her, though, he patted her leg absently and got to work.

Lorna smiled. *Maybe, just maybe,* she thought.

They worked hard for nearly an hour—arguing, finishing each other's sentences and laughing with delight when things began to fall into place.

"This is great, just great," Nick muttered, pounding the keyboard to finish the final paragraph. "Let's end with the quote from the police."

"Why not a quote from Peggy?"

"That's a feature-story way to finish. The police thing gives us the harder edge—the news angle. There. What do you think?"

Lorna leaned over his arm and read the final words. She nodded. "You're right. This is perfect."

Nick glanced at his watch. "Ten minutes to spare. Let's shoot it over to Frank's desk."

He tapped the keys again, sending the story to the computer of the managing editor. Lorna glanced across the newsroom and watched Frank Hoolihan through the window of his office. He noticed the story coming in on his computer and looked up to see Nick and Lorna sitting together at her work station. He seemed to approve and nodded, pulling his screen closer to take a look at the story they had written.

"Here goes nothing," Lorna murmured, crossing her fingers for good luck.

Nick leaned back in his chair and linked his hands behind his head. "Yeah, this can be the tough part—waiting for Frank's response. If it's terrible, he won't come out at all. If it's good, we'll get a few words from him. Maybe even an invitation for drinks."

Lorna looked at Nick. "So we wait?"

He regarded her with a smile. "Yep. Gives us a chance to talk."

"Nick—"

"My turn," he interrupted, keeping his voice low. "I'm an idiot, Cookie, and I know it."

"How about if I give you some time? I know I dropped a bomb on you, and I'm sorry."

Nick shook his head. "Maybe time would help, but I doubt it. For your sake, I think this would work better if we were just friends."

Lorna tried to hold back the rush of sorrow that filled her chest. "Could you do that?" she asked tightly. "After the night in my hotel bed?"

Nick sat up and rustled his hand through the pages of his notes. "That's the tough part," he admitted. "You're a very sexy lady, Cookie. My head spins every time I look at you. Right now I want to peel off that blouse of yours and—" He'd begun to look at her with an obvious hunger in his gaze, but Nick suddenly stopped himself. He laughed shortly. "Well, let's just say the chemistry is still alive and well."

"But you can't get past knowing that I've been raped. Dammit, Nick, *I've* come to terms with it. I've almost put it behind me. Can't you do the same?"

"It's not that easy," he insisted, unfazed by her bluntness. "You've been hurt by somebody and it's taken you two years to get to this point. A couple of days with me can't have done you any good—"

"I wish you'd let me determine what's good or bad for me," Lorna said harshly. *Don't cry,* she told herself. *Don't do it. Just hang on. You've come this far.* She forced her voice to sound civil. "So you want to be just friends, is that it?"

"That would be nice."

"Nice," she repeated wryly. "That's a little better than peachy, isn't it? But not as good as—"

"I'm sorry, Lorna. I never claimed to be an upstanding citizen."

It was unfair. Totally and completely unfair. Just when Lorna started to think she could get on with her life, the past came slamming back again. Only this time it was Nick who had the problem.

Frank Hoolihan was suddenly standing by the desk, appearing like a genie from a bottle, and Nick and Lorna gaped up at him, startled.

Bluntly, Frank said, "Good story. We'll run it on the front page."

Nick grinned and stood up to accept the editor's handshake. "Thanks, Frank."

Frank shook his hand and reached for Lorna's, too. More seriously, he said, "I had no idea how you were connected to this case until I read your story, Miss Kincaid. I think you're mighty brave."

"Thanks," Lorna said. "It's taken me a couple of years to work up the courage, though. That's not very brave."

"Confronting demons is always hard," Frank said. "But the story's terrific."

Nick seemed delighted. "Want to buy us some beer, Frank?"

Frank allowed a grudging smile. "Are you kidding? I'll probably have to spend the whole night talking to our lawyers before the story hits the street tomorrow. By the way, how do you want the byline to read?"

"Both of us," Nick replied, then sent Lorna a twinkle of a grin. "But my name on top, of course."

She smiled a little, not feeling very happy. "Just use Nick's name," she said to Frank. "I'm bringing charges against Angelino myself."

"Lorna—"

"I have to do it. I promised Peggy, and I don't want my connection to this story to mess that up."

"I can't take the credit for this story, Lorna."

"Call it my going-away present to you, Nick."

"Hang on," Frank said, perhaps not noticing the way Nick's expression died. "Let's compromise and make up a name. Lorna Fortune, maybe?"

"Definitely not that," she snapped. "But Nick Kincaid sounds okay."

"That's it, then. See you two later." Frank started for his office, then turned back. "Oh, if you really feel like celebrating, the boys from the sports desk just went out to Frannie Kay's."

"What's Frannie Kay's?" Lorna asked when Frank had departed.

"A dance hall," Nick replied, picking up Lorna's bag and pushing it into her hands. "You'll love it."

"I don't feel like dancing, Nick."

"Me, neither," he said, taking her arm and propelling her toward the elevator. "But it beats hanging around here feeling like a jerk."

* * *

Nick wasn't sure why he wanted Lorna to meet some of his friends. Maybe he thought they'd make her understand what he couldn't manage to convey—that he wasn't a man who ought to settle into a meaningful relationship with any woman, let alone one who had a complex past to deal with.

Frannie Kay's place—a combination rodeo bar and rib joint—was located in a crummy section of Dallas just a five-minute drive from *The Bulletin,* hence its popularity with reporters. Nick left his pickup parked around the corner and escorted a very quiet Lorna through the front door and into the rockabilly bedlam of Frannie's.

Lorna clapped both hands over her ears to shut out some of the noise. Her eyes were round as she looked up at Nick. "What *is* this place?"

Nick shrugged. "A hangout. Not a bad place to pick up pretty tourists to tell the truth, but—"

"What?" she shouted, squinting to read his lips in the smoke-filled, strobe-lighted darkness. "I can't hear a word you're saying!"

"Never mind."

"What?"

"I said— Oh, the hell with it."

He took her elbow, having spotted Lenny, Cassandra and Patrick from the sports desk. His friends had staked a claim on a stretch of the bar and were drinking tequila and beer while consuming vast quantities of peanuts and hot wings with celery—a combination considered quite nutritious among deadline-pressed journalists. Across the room, a band was already playing—two guitars, a fiddle and an electronic keyboard with a couple of wailing singers dressed in cowboy duds. In between, the dance floor was already filling up with people who had just finished working downtown, but weren't ready to go home just yet.

"This way," Nick bellowed in Lorna's ear, guiding her toward his friends.

The sportswriters were regular customers at Frannie's, and they had long ago discovered exactly which spot at the bar was acoustically right for conversation. They raised their glasses to salute Nick, and seemed pleased to meet Lorna.

"My, my, you sure are a pretty little filly," Patrick drawled when they were introduced. "Glad to make your acquaintance, Miz Kincaid."

"Don't believe the cowpoke routine," Nick said to her. "Patrick's from Philadelphia."

"Aw, shucks," Patrick said, grinning. "You never let me get away with anything, Nickie."

Cassandra gave Lorna one of her patented firm handshakes and a sisterly wink. "Great to meet you," she said to Lorna. "Seeing much of Nick?"

"Not much," Lorna replied with a forced smile. "He can't handle me."

Cassandra laughed, and so did Lenny as he took Lorna's hand and said with the oily smile of a matinee idol, "How about a two-step, Lorna?"

"What's a two-step?"

Lenny waggled his eyebrows and spun her around expertly. "I was once a dance instructor—and a good one. Let me show you."

She laughed, looking a little happier. "I'm game. Let's go."

Lenny whisked her off to the dance floor, and Cassandra said to Nick, "Dance instructor? That's a new one! He's a real Lothario, Nick. You'd better cut in if you want to keep her."

Nick leaned on the bar and signaled Frannie for a beer. "Oh, let Lenny do his stuff for a while."

Cassandra turned and leaned on the bar next to him, and Patrick filled the space on Nick's other side. Together, they hemmed him in for a pow-wow. The three of them had become good friends during their years at *The Bulletin.* Patrick's divorce had been the first cataclysm that brought them together, and Cassandra's bout with breast cancer had also caused the threesome to do quite a bit of carousing—first to "make hay while the sun shines," as Cassandra said herself, and later to celebrate her first and second cancer-free years. There wasn't anybody in Dallas Nick trusted more. Lenny, who occasionally joined the group, was also a friend, but not nearly the same kind the other two were.

Patrick said, "So who is she, Nickie? She's gorgeous."

"Somebody passing through, that's all. A short-term reporter Hoolihan brought in."

"A short-term reporter you spent the night with two nights ago?" Cassandra guessed with a wry grin. "When I called your place at midnight to give you some free tickets to the ball game, you were out."

"Who says I spent the night with anyone?"

"Me," Cassandra said. She liked to think of herself as a tough-talking broad, one of the boys. "I tried the newsroom, too, and they said you were with a drop-dead blonde from back East. I put two and two together, and it adds up to a hot night in *some*body's bed."

Nick grabbed his beer from Frannie's hand and got busy slugging it down while his friends exchanged significant looks over his head.

"Dish the dirt, Nickie," Patrick said, elbowing him. "Are you really seeing her? As in dating, I mean? As in sleeping together?"

"What's so crazy about it if I was?"

"Nothing," Patrick said quickly. "Not a thing, right, Cass?"

"Nothing at all," Cassandra agreed. "She doesn't look like your soul mate, exactly, but that's good. That could be very good, in fact."

"What's that supposed to mean?"

Cassandra sipped her tequila. "Well, Nickie, you're an unusual guy. You need a woman who—well, somebody who'll give you a kick in the pants now and then."

"Somebody who'll make you get your hair cut," Patrick added. "No offense, of course."

"Of course," Nick cracked, getting irritated with all the meddling he had hoped would be directed at Lorna, not himself. "Some women like my hair the way it is, you know."

"Bag ladies," Cassandra said, laughing. "No offense, of course. Look, Nickie, sometimes a guy uses just about anything to prevent a real relationship from breaking out, you know? Take it from me, I've seen all the possibilities, and you're a prime example. I mean, your clothes, the food you eat, the way you keep your apartment—"

"I hired a housekeeper last year, I'll have you know."

"A step in the right direction," Cassandra said approvingly. "But the rest of the package is a way of keeping women at arm's length."

"Lorna doesn't say a word about the way I dress."

"So far," Patrick predicted. "Have you tried to get into a real restaurant in that T-shirt?"

"Well, no, but—"

"I think you're going to have to invest in a tie at long last, Nickie. She doesn't look like the fast-food type to me," Patrick said.

"She isn't."

"Well, it's time you became an adult in that department, anyway. I'll take you to a couple of shops over the weekend. We'll get you suited up in no time."

Patrick was a notorious clotheshorse, but unfortunately, his off-the-job tastes ran to fringed shirts, string ties, rat-stabber boots and very expensive hats. As politely as possible, Nick said, "Uh, no thanks, Pat."

"Look, Nickie," Cassandra said, patting his hand, "we're your friends, right? Tell us the truth. Do you like this Kincaid person?"

"Sure."

"How much?"

"A lot," Nick said in all honesty.

"Is she smart?"

"Yes."

"Funny?"

"Yeah, lots of fun."

Bluntly, Patrick said, "Is she good in bed?"

Nick felt himself get hot. "Now look—"

"That means yes," Cassandra said smugly, "but he's still a Texas gentleman and won't tattle. So she's got everything, right? Plus she's good-looking. I've got a great feeling about this one, and you know how good my radar is."

"What radar? You only talked to her for three seconds!"

"I can tell. Trust me. She's exactly what you need."

Point is, I'm the last thing *she* needs, Nick thought.

"I can tell she's got class," Cassandra continued. "Look, it's practically spray-painted on her forehead. What are you waiting for, Nick?"

"Look." Patrick spun around, rested his arms on the bar and leaned back to watch the dancers. "In five minutes, Lenny is going to have her phone number. In ten minutes, he's going to— Well, you know what Lenny is capable of."

Nick turned around and watched as his old buddy Lenny Carrera held Lorna close and two-stepped her around the dance floor, murmuring who-knew-what-nonsense into her ear and making her laugh. She stumbled once or twice, but she'd caught on to the dance easily, and Lenny's whip-thin body seemed a perfect shadow to hers. Her pretty mouth was curved into one of her delightful smiles, and her hair swung beautifully in time with the music.

"Damn," Nick said, under his breath. His heart felt weird all of a sudden. Here was a complicated woman. And he wanted her. But he was scared.

Yeah, scared, said his inner voice. *You have no idea how to handle this.*

"Do something," Cassandra said, prodding him with her elbow. "Dance with her."

"It's not that simple, Cass."

"*Make* it simple," she advised. "That woman could be good for you, Nickie."

"Uh-oh," said Patrick. "Now what?"

A reeling drunk in a crooked cowboy hat had launched himself off the bar and was staggering in the direction of Lenny and Lorna. He planted himself directly in their path. Although Nick couldn't hear what was said, it was obvious that the drunk wanted to dance with Lorna.

"Oh, hell," Nick said, just as the drunk swung a punch and landed it right on Lenny's jaw. Lenny dropped over backward like a felled ox. Lorna clapped both hands over her mouth to stifle a scream.

"Here goes nothing," Nick said.

He reached the drunk just as the man seized Lorna's hand. Grabbing the cowboy's shoulder, Nick spun him around and punched the guy between the eyes. Lorna cried out and jumped back as the drunk fell on the floor, knocked out cold.

Cassandra and Patrick reached Lenny's side to render aid. Cassandra took the time to throw Nick a blinding grin and yell, "Get her out of here, Nickie! Before somebody arrests you!"

Nick decided to take Cassandra's advice.

Eight

____

Driving his truck again through the dark city streets, Lorna found herself muttering. "Of all the grand-standing, saloon-brawling, cowboy foolishness! I can't believe you hit that poor kid."

"He was not a kid," Nick growled from the passenger seat, clumsily holding a bar towel filled with melting ice against his right hand. "And I was defending your honor, not brawling."

"My honor was not in question," Lorna snapped, although she felt anything but angry. In fact, Nick's rush to her defense was rather charming—unless he had managed to break his knuckles in the process. Holding in a smile, she said, "The emergency-room doctor is going to start wondering about you."

"We're not going to any emergency room!"

"Nick! Your hand is actually bleeding—don't deny it," she said as he began to protest. "I saw it. You shouldn't risk an injury. If you couldn't use a computer keyboard—"

"I'm not going to the hospital."

His tone was final, so Lorna shut up. Nick was perfectly capable of deciding his own fate.

"Take me home," he said, still grouchy. "Turn left at this light."

Lorna obeyed, and it wasn't until they'd traveled several blocks that she realized she might actually be invited to see his apartment. And that she was either going to have to hire a cab to get to her hotel or drive the pickup back herself.

Or spend the night with Nick.

She felt pretty sure he wasn't going to invite her, though. She began to wonder how he'd toss her out.

"Another left up here," Nick said when Lorna's imagination was in full swing. "I wasn't grandstanding."

"What?"

"At Frannie's. I wasn't grandstanding."

"Okay, okay, let's forget it."

"But I didn't do it for fun, either, you know."

"I said forget it, didn't I?"

He grumbled under his breath—something about ungrateful women, which Lorna chose to ignore. She hadn't asked him to come to her rescue, after all. Punching a stranger over a silly dance request was downright medieval—or Texan, perhaps, but what was the difference?

"Up ahead," Nick said at last. "See those gates? Go through there. Take it slow."

"Wow," Lorna said in spite of herself as she drove his rattletrap pickup through a pair of enormous wrought-iron gates more suited to a Cotswold manor house than a Dallas apartment building. "I thought you said you had an apartment. This is some kind of estate."

"No, it's an old pump station for the water company."

Cleverly placed spotlights illuminated the brick building, which was round and decorated with various curved windows and even a gargoyle or two. Upon driving closer, Lorna saw that it had certainly served an industrial purpose once, but now the power lines had been cleared away, leaving a rather pretty building about the size of a large barn but much more elaborate.

"This is really your place?"

"Not exactly. An architect friend of mine bought it from the city a couple of years ago. He's renovating the building and living in part of the space. I'm paying a little rent to help pay for fixing up the old place, but he'll eventually throw me out—when he can afford it. Turn here and park."

Nick pointed to a cul de sac where an expensive German-made car had been parked. Lorna pulled alongside it, but didn't shut off the engine or headlights.

Nick climbed out of the truck and slammed the door gingerly with his sore hand. "This way," he called.

She could have left. To save them both the embarrassment, she could have bid Nick good-night and gone back to her hotel. But she was curious. Very curious to see how Nick lived.

So Lorna shut off the engine and followed hesitantly. The brick path to his door had been carefully laid in a decorative swirl, and small Oriental lamps and attractive desert plants had been strategically placed along its curves for a Japanese-garden effect. Up ahead, Nick unlocked a large wooden door—one that looked as if it might have been salvaged from an ancient Mexican mission, perhaps—and reached inside to flip on a light. Then he pushed the door wide and allowed Lorna to enter first.

"It might be a little messy," Nick warned. "But it's clean under the clutter, honest."

The entry was laid with cool tiles, and a leather jacket hung from a wooden peg by the door. Three wide steps led down to a sunken living space where someone had made an attempt to decorate the place in art deco. Two leather couches, a leggy black lacquer table, a single lamp with frosted-glass leaves for a shade—they all made an attractive picture, except Nick had managed to scatter evidence of his work all over the place. Newspapers, magazines, a laptop computer seemed to cover every horizontal surface.

A wide stone staircase led upward to a loft. And Nick's bedroom, Lorna decided.

Opposite the staircase, a long bar that had been covered with a mosaic of broken colored tile separated the living room from the kitchen, which looked small, but functional. Nick had left his microwave oven standing open, and the feeble light illuminated a countertop free of dirty dishes, but cluttered with a telephone, unopened mail and a grocery bag with assorted canned goods spilling out.

Looking at the beautiful, spare lines of the room and the clean, sparse decoration, Lorna decided that Nick had done what any sane person would do. He had softened his harsh quarters, made them comfortable in his own way.

"You picked the furniture?" she asked.

"Nope," Nick replied, not surprising her. He had closed the door and come down the steps after her, pocketing his keys. "I had a girlfriend once who wanted to be an interior decorator. She did most of this."

Lorna strolled deeper into the living room and was startled to see a black cat sleeping on one of the couches. "That's yours?" she asked, pointing.

"Uh, no," Nick said, fixing himself a drink with his good hand. "He belongs to Hal, my architect friend, but he seems to spend most of his time over here. I don't know why. All he does is sleep. His name is Sugar Ray."

The cat didn't even open an eye to acknowledge their arrival.

Lorna glanced up at Nick and found him standing very still and staring at her oddly. His ice cubes, momentarily forgotten, were dripping on the tile floor. She said, "Something wrong?"

He shook himself. "No, nothing. I just—well, I'll call you a cab. You must be tired."

"Not really." Lorna wasn't ready to leave. Not yet. "Why don't we have a look at your hand?"

In the kitchen, they cautiously peeled the bar towel off Nick's knuckles, revealing some scrapes and a large, smeary bruise starting.

Lorna probed gently and asked, "You're sure nothing's broken?"

"I didn't hit him very hard."

"It looked hard."

Nick allowed Lorna to dry his hand with a paper towel. "I guess it was a pretty stupid move."

"Very," Lorna agreed, then looked up into his eyes. "But a little romantic."

"Romantic?" He laughed, amazed. "How do you figure that?"

"You must actually care about me," she said bravely. "If you're fighting off obnoxious drunks and rescuing me from the lecherous arms of your friend Lenny."

Nick began to glare again. "Was he being lecherous? Why, I'll track him down and—"

"Now, now," Lorna said, patting his chest. "Look what trouble that kind of thinking got you into tonight."

"Yeah," Nick said, suddenly gazing deeply into Lorna's face and bringing his left hand up to touch the small of her back. Her own hand was still resting on his chest where she was sure she could feel his heartbeat start to accelerate. In a different tone, Nick murmured, "Look where it got me."

"I'm glad you stepped in, Nick. It was unnecessary, maybe, but very gallant."

"Gallant, huh?" he echoed, looking far from attentive to their conversation. He seemed mesmerized by the sight of her lips.

"Thank you," she whispered, but she was sure he didn't hear.

Nick bent closer, as if pulled by a magnet, and Lorna rose to meet him. The kiss started gentle, but Lorna soon arched her body against his and slipped her arms around his neck. She couldn't help herself. In another moment, Nick was holding her tightly against himself. Her breasts were soft on his chest, her thighs pliant against his. She was being foolish—crazy, maybe—but it was thrilling to be in his arms again.

Nick broke the kiss at last and began nuzzling her throat, groaning. "This isn't supposed to be happening."

"I don't think we can stop."

"Lorna—"

"I know," she whispered, emotion catching in her throat. "I know how you feel."

He didn't want emotional involvement. He couldn't handle her past and didn't feel up to helping her overcome it. But Lorna didn't care—at that moment. Tonight all she wanted was to have him with her again. Damn it all, he made her feel good. And seeing where he lived, meeting his friends, working on the story with him had made Nick Fortune even more appealing. Whether he knew it or not...he did care. And so did Lorna.

As he began caressing her through her blouse, Nick said, "We shouldn't do this. It's not fair."

"Life isn't always fair."

In just a few minutes, they were upstairs in his bedroom, and Nick was undressing Lorna with rushed excitement. Her own fingers were clumsy on his belt, but they managed to strip him naked in no time. Nick opened a drawer and found the all-important protection. Then Lorna pulled Nick down onto the rumpled bed, and they made love quickly, without the preliminaries of before. The climax was the same, however— explosive and powerful.

Afterward, Lorna thought she ought to be crying. But she found herself deliriously happy. Nestled in his bed, stroking Nick's rough cheek and looking languidly into his dark eyes, she wondered why on earth she should be feeling so damn content with a man who didn't want to be with her.

Or so he claimed.

She longed to tell him how she felt—how quickly she'd fallen for him despite his shortcomings.

I should never have told him what happened to me. That thought spun relentlessly in her head. If only she'd kept quiet, they could have had a future together. She felt sure of that. But Lorna wasn't good at lying.

"What's the matter?" he asked, husky-voiced. "Your eyes just changed."

She closed them and shook her head. "Nothing." She didn't want to talk. It would only spoil things. If Nick wasn't ready to accept Lorna the way she was, chances were he never would.

The telephone rang before Nick could press her further.

Left-handed, Nick fumbled with the receiver and brought it to his ear. "Yeah?"

Lorna couldn't hear the voice on the other end of the line, but she felt Nick tense.

"Yeah," he said. "I know where she is."

The rapid-voice began to talk, filling Nick's ear with information that made his pulse jump under her caressing fingertips. He sat up in the bed, dragging the sheet with him as he reached for the lamp. When light filled the small room, he grabbed a pad and pen from the night stand. "Okay, Frank," he said. "Give me what you have."

Lorna sat up, too, and reached for the nearest article of clothing—Nick's T-shirt. She slipped it over her head and was ready to listen once Nick hung up the phone.

"Well?"

"You won't believe it." Nick's expression was alive with excitement. "Angelino got wind of our article. His lawyers have already called Frank to block the story."

"Frank's still going to run it, isn't he?"

"Yep. In fact, he wants us to get a quote from Angelino ourselves."

"Do we call him?"

Shaking his head, Nick said, "No way. He won't take our calls. We have to catch him someplace. And Frank says he's scheduled to attend a reception at the Derrick Club tomorrow."

"We catch him there?"

"Frank's gotta get us some tickets. It's a closed affair, very posh. Black-tie."

"Can Frank do that?"

"Frank can do anything. He's wired all over town." Pleased and excited, Nick leaned back against the pillow again and reached, without thinking, to stroke Lorna's bare thigh.

Lorna didn't notice his touch. Her brain was seething, too. "The right quote could ruin Angelino, couldn't it, Nick?"

"You bet. We'll have to plan this carefully."

"He could incriminate himself, couldn't he? If he said the wrong thing, right?"

"You bet."

Lorna seized Nick's hand. "Let's call your friend Washington."

"Why?" Nick looked startled.

"He wanted someone to wear a wire, Nick. That's what he said when Peggy and I first went to see him. They want Angelino to spill his guts, but they know he won't do it when they drag him into the station. If one of us spoke to him at the reception—got him alone, maybe, and coaxed him into saying something about his actions at Harborside—"

"Wearing a wire is a lot like entrapment. It takes a seasoned cop to do it right. Maybe Washington has someone—"

"A woman."

Nick snapped his fingers. "Yes, a woman. Perfect."

"Call him. Right now, call Washington and ask him."

"You call him," Nick said with a laugh. "He'll probably hang up on me."

It felt great to be working with Nick again. There were no emotional barriers. Lorna reached for the telephone, but Nick stopped her with one hand under her chin. He tipped her face up to his gently. "Cookie," he said. "You're something else."

Lorna returned his smile. "I could call Washington in the morning, couldn't I?"

Nick smiled deeply into her eyes, and in that moment Lorna knew he understood she didn't want to break the spell of their night together. "Sure," he murmured. "Washington will still be around in the morning."

Lorna hoped Nick would be, too.

Orville Washington was the kind of cop who made good men glad they weren't criminals, Nick decided the next morning. Just watching Washington crush a foam coffee cup and hurl it into the nearest trash can caused Nick to give thanks he had never seriously considered a life of crime.

"'Morning, Washington."

"Get the hell away from my desk, Fortune. You know how I feel about the press."

"You talk to Miss Kincaid," Nick protested. "She's the press, too."

"She's a nice lady," Washington said, actually pulling out a dented office chair for Lorna. "She deserves my respect. You, on the other hand—"

"I get the picture." Nick was very glad he'd come to the station with Lorna. He was even happier that he'd awakened in her arms just an hour earlier and enjoyed toast and coffee with her in his kitchen. Lorna had a nice smile in the morning, and a gentle way of waking up—no breathless rush to shower and put on her makeup. He boosted himself up on the next nearest desk and prepared to listen to the cops who had gathered around.

While Nick and Lorna listened, the cops quickly got down to business, making plans for the arrest of Martin Angelino.

"We should wait another day to be on the safe side," Washington growled. "To get statements from more of the women at Harborside. But because *The Bulletin* has run their freaking story in this morning's edition, I guess we have to grab the guy today."

"Before this reception thing?" asked one of the cops. "Like, how come we don't ride over there right now and pick up the bum?"

"We figure he'll stick around town for the reception," said Washington. "He's getting some kind of award for donating to a charity. What a racket that is. Anyway, we want to get him to say a few words to Mr. Edison before we pick him up."

Lorna leaned forward curiously. "Mr. Edison?"

"To a tape recorder," Washington explained, the picture of politeness.

Lorna nodded, satisfied. She looked even better than usual this morning, Nick decided, and all the cops had noticed, too. There was a glow to her skin, a certain fathomless beauty to her eyes. She looked like a woman who had been well-loved the night before, a woman who had cast aside all her inhibitions for a satisfying night of erotic fun and games, a woman who—

"What are you grinning about, Fortune?" Washington demanded, catching sight of Nick's face.

"Uh, nothing. Go ahead, Washington."

"Damn-fool reporters," Washington grumbled before going ahead with the meeting.

About half an hour later, when the meeting broke up, Nick captured Lorna's hand and pulled her out of the station house. They walked back to *The Bulletin*, a distance of less than three blocks.

"Did Frank get us tickets to the reception?" Lorna asked, unaware of Nick's fantasy that maybe they ought to take a run down to the ocean for a couple of days. "Did he, Nick?"

"Yep. Starts at five o'clock."

"Great." She checked her watch. "That gives us a few hours to find some clothes."

"Find some clothes?" Nick repeated, snapping back to reality. "What do you mean?"

"I checked your closet this morning," Lorna said with a smile. "And I didn't notice a dinner jacket among all your T-shirts."

"Because I don't own one."

"Every man should own a dinner jacket, Nick." She spoke with the absolute certainty of a woman whose assorted family members had reported society weddings for decades. "This city has the most wonderful department stores. I'm sure we can find something formal for you to wear."

"Now wait a minute—"

"And I certainly didn't bring a dress that would be suitable for the reception." She steamrolled sweetly over his protests. "Will you help me pick out a dress, Nick?"

The mental image of Lorna standing half-naked in a dressing room while Nick stood by ready to zip zippers or button buttons was suddenly too delicious to ignore. Nick's mouth actually began to water at the idea.

But he managed to shake his head. "I'd love to," he said with real regret, "but I have things to do."

"Something important?"

"Very."

Lorna stopped on the sidewalk. "That sounds mysterious. Is it something I should know about?"

He grasped her shoulders with both hands and squeezed, wishing he could tell the truth. "Not yet. I'll pick up a tux myself, okay? And I'll meet you at your hotel at four-thirty, in time to go to the reception."

"Nick—"

"Trust me," he said, giving Lorna a quick kiss on her forehead. "I'll see you then."

He grabbed a cab and rode with a chatty driver who wanted to discuss Troy Aikman's future as an all-time great quarterback. Nick listened with only half an ear, but paid the fare and added an extra buck on the tip when he disembarked at the Women's Free Film Institute.

At the carefully guarded door, Nick was once again greeted by the very tall Marcy Hendricks, who recognized him but was unwilling to allow him into the building without Lorna along to hold his leash, it seemed.

"No appointment, no admittance," Marcy said firmly.

"I was hoping to talk to Peggy."

"About what?"

Nick considered several wisecrack answers, but ended up saying, "Something personal. Would you mind telling her I'm here? I'll wait outside, if you'd like. Just tell her I'd like a chance to talk."

Marcy looked him over from her great height once again, perhaps trying to guess if he was carrying a bomb or maybe an updated copy of *Joe Bob's Drive-in Movie Guide* featuring the best car chase, decapitation and chain saw movies of all time. But Nick must have managed to appear benign, because Marcy suddenly nodded and closed the door in his face.

Five minutes later, she came back with permission to enter the secured halls.

"Peggy says she'll see you. But I'll come along."

"Look, I'm only going to talk to her."

Marcy led the way. "That's good."

Nick debated whether or not he should suggest that if Marcy ever lost her job at the film institute, she could probably get work as a knee breaker for the Mob. But he'd sustained quite enough injuries in the past few days to risk any further bodily harm, so he kept his mouth shut.

Peggy wasn't in the film editing lab anymore, but had placed herself behind a very large desk in the office across the hall. When Nick arrived, she didn't stand up or extend her hand, just sat still and looked nervous.

"Thanks for seeing me," Nick said at once, hoping to put her at ease. "It's generous of you to give me some of your time."

"Marcy mentioned it was personal," Peggy said in her soft, barely audible voice. "I thought it might involve Lorna."

"It does," Nick said, glancing at Marcy.

Marcy took the hint. To Peggy, she said, "I'll wait outside. Want me to leave the door open?"

Peggy shook her head, and in another moment, they were alone in the small office together. Nick sat down in a spindly director's chair in front of Peggy's desk. He folded his hands in his lap, but felt silly, so he put them on the arms of the chair. That felt worse, so he set his hands on his knees. The chair was the most awkward piece of furniture he'd ever sat in.

Peggy began to smile. "You look uncomfortable."

Feeling sheepish, Nick said, "I don't know how to start."

"You said it involves Lorna."

"In a way, yes. Mostly, it's about me."

Peggy's eyebrows shot up. "You?"

Nick felt like a fool. But he wanted answers. "I need some help," he said slowly. "Some advice, I guess. I thought maybe you could— Well, I need some insight into a problem—Lorna's problem. No, that's not right. It's my problem."

Watching him with growing interest, Peggy leaned forward and put her elbows on the desk, the first body language that communicated her willingness to listen. "How do you think I can help?"

Nick got up out of the instrument of torture that was supposed to be a chair and tried to pace. The office was too small, however, so he ended up shoving his hands into the front pockets of his jeans and standing in one place. "I've gotten to know Lorna pretty well," he said to Peggy, who listened politely. "In fact, we got to know each other *really* well, if you know what I mean, and it was—well, maybe you don't want to hear that part."

"The sex," Peggy said softly. "You enjoyed it?"

Nick gulped, wondering if this trip was going to cause more harm than good. But he'd come this far. He might as well go the distance. "We both did. A lot. But afterward, Lorna told me what happened between her and Martin Angelino."

"She hadn't explained it before?"

Nick shook his head. "Not even a hint. Believe me, I was blown away. I had no idea. She seemed so..."

"Normal?" Peggy finished.

"I'm sorry. I'm being stupid, aren't I?" Suddenly, Nick decided he shouldn't have come. He was only making things worse for everyone. "I didn't mean to upset you. I just— Listen, I'll just go—"

"Please don't," Peggy said, raising her voice for the first time. The sound seemed to startle even herself. She smiled again and said, "Really, I'd like to help."

"I don't mean to insult you."

"I can't help what happened to me," she said, looking composed. "So let's talk."

Nick sat down again and sighed heavily. "The thing is, I really like her. I was starting to think Lorna and I could be more than just friends, in fact. I thought there was something special between us."

"And telling you about the rape has changed that?"

"No. Yes. I mean— Hell, that's what I've come to you about. I don't know how to deal with it!"

Peggy looked grave. "There are some good therapists around. And support groups. There's one run by the center where I stayed—"

"No, no, I don't think there's time for that. She's only here for a little while, and I—I'm afraid I'm going to lose her before I figure out what to do."

"You must like her a lot."

"I do."

"Maybe it's more than liking."

"What do you mean?"

Peggy's smile grew affectionate. "You're a tough nut to crack, aren't you?"

"If you mean am I falling in love with her, I can't answer that. I was married once, and if that was love, it's not what I feel for Lorna—"

"There are lots of kinds of love."

"Maybe." Once again, Nick started to feel foolish. "But I— Look, I just came to find out what I ought to say to her, what I ought to do. I feel so helpless!"

"There aren't any rules about these situations, you know."

"Being supportive," he said heavily, "isn't my strong suit."

"What is?"

"Pardon?"

"What is your strong suit? Where Lorna is concerned, that is? Why does she like you?"

"I don't know if she does."

"She does." Peggy nodded decisively. "We both know that. What's so special about you?"

Nick shrugged. "I dunno. I showed her a good time, I guess."

"That's it?"

"Yeah, we have fun together."

"Maybe that's it. Maybe she's attracted to you because you're fun." When Nick looked exasperated, Peggy said patiently, "I have an inkling about what the past two years have been like for Lorna. Mind you, everybody's different and we handle things in our own ways, but I think Lorna's probably had enough tea and sympathy. She's ready to put the past behind her, and you're the first step."

"I'm not sure I want to be the first step in recovery. I'd rather..."

"Yes? What *do* you want, Nick?"

He sighed. "For things to be easy, I guess."

"Don't we all," she said with a small laugh. "But maybe they can be. Maybe you ought to just hang in there and see what happens."

"But..."

"Yes?"

"What should I do?" he asked. "What should I say? I don't know how to act! We're going to see Angelino this afternoon, and I don't know what to expect."

"Lorna's going to see him?"

Nodding, Nick said, "It's inevitable. We're going to talk to him before he's arrested. It's bound to be difficult for Lorna."

Peggy sat back. "You're right. I haven't seen him since he—well, I've avoided him. I'd be afraid to face him. I'm not sure why. I just don't want to ever lay eyes on him again." Involuntarily, she shivered.

"Lorna must feel the same way."

Peggy nodded uneasily. "Maybe so."

"What should I do? Make her stay in her hotel?"

"You can't make her do anything."

"Okay, but—"

"Look, I can't guess how Lorna's feeling."

"You can't help?"

"Do you really want my advice?" Peggy said. "Just love her, Nick."

Nick wasn't so sure that was enough, and his expression must have shown that opinion.

Peggy said, "Your first step ought to be talking to her. Instead of baring your soul to me, why not open up to Lorna? It may upset her, but you're going to have to take that risk, I think, if you want to keep her in your life."

Nine

Lorna paced around her hotel suite in her dressy clothes and tried to decide how she felt about seeing Martin Angelino for the first time in two years.

Scared? Definitely.

But there were other emotions boiling around inside her, too. She'd come a long way. She was a survivor. Lorna smiled at that thought. Sure, she'd had a bad experience. One of the worst a woman could face. But look where she was right now. On track and ready to take on the world.

With luck, she intended to take on Nick Fortune, too.

Where is he, by the way? It's getting late.

As if on cue, a knock sounded at her door, and Lorna flew across the carpet in her stocking feet to answer it.

"Nick, I was starting to get worried— Oh, it's you."

Detective Washington stood in the hallway, dressed in a spiffy pinstripe suit and looking surprisingly well-groomed without his bandanna. "'Evening, Miss Kincaid. Nick's been held up—something about a tuxedo, he said. He asked me to take you to the reception."

"He's coming, isn't he?" Lorna felt panicked at the thought of facing Angelino without Nick by her side.

"Sure, he's coming. He's just having trouble with his cummerbund, I guess. You ready to go?"

"Let me get my shoes."

Five minutes later Lorna was riding down to the street in the hotel elevator with Washington.

Perhaps the police officer guessed her state of mind, because he began to talk as they walked out to the unmarked car. "I want you to know how much we appreciate your help in this case, Miss Kincaid."

"I'm glad to do it," she said absently.

"It takes guts, though."

"I must admit, I'm a little nervous about seeing Angelino face-to-face. And pressing charges—it's got me scared."

"Understandable." Washington held the car door open for her, and Lorna got inside. A moment later he got in, too, and started the car and the air conditioner.

Lorna fastened her seat belt. "I'm glad you agreed to help us through this, Detective Washington. I know this kind of thing isn't your regular assignment."

He grinned and ran his thumb under the lapel of his suit jacket. "Beats shooting at drug dealers."

She smiled. "I'm glad you're here."

He drove easily, instinctively watching the street and sidewalk as they traveled uptown toward the reception. At last, he said, "The plan is for Detective Rogers to wear a wire to the reception. You met her at the station, right? She's going to try to get Angelino to in-

FORTUNE'S COOKIE 157

criminate himself on tape before we arrest him. Rogers is a pro. She'll do okay."

"Great."

But when they arrived at the hotel where the charity reception was to take place, Washington received some bad news.

"Sorry, sir," said a uniformed cop who met them at the hotel door and drew them aside. "But Detective Rogers has been detained."

Washington took the news poorly. "Where the hell is she, dammit?"

"Her son got hit by a car while riding his bike on the street. He's at the emergency room—"

"Kevin? Kevin's hurt?"

"I hear it's not too bad, sir. He was wearing a helmet. Just some bruises and maybe a broken arm. But Rogers can't leave him for at least a couple of hours."

"And by that time," Washington growled, "this freaking reception will be over. Damn! Now what are we supposed to do?"

The hotel lobby was thronged with incoming reception guests, all dressed in Texas finery and looking beautiful. Lorna stood slightly behind Washington and watched the crowd—keeping a particular eye out for Nick.

And Martin Angelino.

Suddenly she saw him.

The sight of the man hit her like a punch to the stomach. It paralyzed her. It turned her blood to ice.

He was with two women—both young, lovely and dressed in expensive clothing and jewelry. Angelino himself had put on a few pounds and maybe lost a little of the dark hair around his temples. In his tuxedo, he looked like an important man, all right—tanned, sure of himself and laughing.

Lorna expected to be afraid of him. He had certainly haunted her nightmares for many months. But suddenly, watching as he stepped onto the escalator and began the ride upward, she didn't feel frightened.

She felt great.

By nightfall, Martin Angelino was going to be in jail. And she was going to help put him there. She wasn't his victim anymore. That had been a lifetime ago. Now she was her own person—and nobody could take that away from her ever again.

"Detective Washington," she said suddenly. "I have an idea."

He listened, but protested as soon as the proposal was out of Lorna's mouth. "We can't have you do that, Miss Kincaid."

"Why not? Rogers can't get here in time. And besides, she didn't know Angelino. What did you expect him to say to a woman he doesn't know? That's not his style. But he'll remember me. Better yet, he'll *talk* to me. Let me wear the wire."

"The department's policy—"

"Oh, come on! I'm not in any danger here!"

"We can't protect you adequately."

"What could he do to me in this hotel with all his friends around? The worst that could happen is that I'll get a drink thrown in my face."

"What about entrapment?"

"All I can do is try!"

"She's right, sir," the uniformed cop said. "She could help. It wouldn't be the first time we got a little assistance from the press."

Washington's face was set. "Do you know how much I hate the press?"

"Let me try to change your mind," Lorna begged. "Please, let me talk to Angelino. There's nobody in this hotel who wants him convicted more than I do."

"Except me," Nick said, coming up at that moment.

He was almost unrecognizable in an elegant dinner jacket and tie. He'd gotten a haircut and shaved, and he looked more like the picture of a cosmopolitan journalist—casual and smooth. Of course, his earring was still in place—and it twinkled with devilry. He glanced from Lorna to Washington and back again. "What's going on?"

"Who the hell are you?" Washington asked.

"Wise guy. Hey, Cookie."

Lorna reached up on tiptoe to kiss his smoothly shaven cheek. "You look like Prince Charming. Positively suave."

"Prince Charming isn't supposed to be late. Sorry about that. The tailor at the store needed a little encouragement to get the alterations done in time, then my truck died. I had to borrow some wheels. Do you like it? The monkey suit, I mean."

"It's fabulous."

"I figured I might need a suit like this," he said, smiling down at her. "If I'm going to be hanging out with a lady like you."

Lorna's heart turned over. "Oh, Nick."

"Oh, Nick," said Washington, sarcastic and impatient.

"I'm sorry," Lorna said then. "Nick, listen, I—"

"Something fishy is going on," he said, eyeing the police. "What is it?"

"Our officer can't make it," Washington said baldly. "So your friend here has volunteered to talk to Angelino herself."

"Forget it," Nick said promptly, suddenly no longer at ease. "She can't do it. You can't, Lorna."

"Why not?"

"Because I don't want you near that guy! You shouldn't have to face him at all—not after what he did to you."

"I want to do it, Nick."

Mimicking her, Washington said, "She wants to do it, Nick."

"Shut up." Nick's face turned dark. "Both of you, just shut up! I won't let you do it, Lorna."

"It's not your decision," Lorna snapped. "Quit trying to baby-sit me."

"What are you trying to prove? How tough you are?"

"I want him in jail, Nick. And I can put him there. If you can't watch, then go home."

"I'm staying," Nick retorted. "As long as you're here, I'm here."

"Great," Washington said. "Just don't chase him down the street this time, okay?"

With the uniformed officer, Lorna stepped outside the hotel and climbed into the back of a large white van. Inside, the vehicle had been stripped and refitted with electronics equipment. Two officers sat with headphones dangling around their necks, and they were playing a halfhearted game of cards.

"Here you go, boys," said the cop. "This young lady needs to be wired for sound."

At the request of the sound men, Lorna took off the jacket to her white linen dinner suit and unbuttoned her silk blouse. She felt awkward while they taped the plastic cord to her bare torso and quickly rebuttoned when they declared they were finished. After she slipped into the jacket again, they planted the microphone in her breast pocket and asked if she had something with which to conceal it. Lorna offered a lace handkerchief from her quilted evening bag, and they tucked it carefully around the microphone before declaring her ready for action.

"You look better than Rogers," one of the sound men said. "She's a good-looking woman, but she's not cut out for high-society stuff. Nobody's going to get suspicious about you, though. You fit right in, miss."

"Thanks. Shall I step outside for a sound check now?"

"Please."

Outside the van, Nick and Washington were arguing loudly enough for Lorna's microphone to pick up the sound perfectly. When she approached, she said, "I'm ready. Let's do it now while my courage is high."

"Lorna, you don't have to do this. You have nothing to prove."

"I know I don't."

"Please," Nick said, catching both her hands in his. "I don't want you to get hurt."

"I'll be fine."

But she wasn't completely sure of that, Lorna decided as the three of them rode the escalator up to the hotel ballroom where the reception was taking place. Watching Angelino from across the lobby was one thing, but actually approaching him, speaking to him— that was something else. As they reached the top of the escalator, she felt a momentary wave of panic, but reached for Nick's hand and felt him instantly squeeze her.

She tipped her head and gave him a tentative smile, asking for something—she wasn't sure what.

Nick looked down at her and said suddenly, "I love you."

Lorna couldn't breathe—didn't dare. It was as if a sudden storm cloud had passed over, hot and unexpected, sucking all the air from her. Nick laughed, his black eyes filling with their unique and dazzling light, giving her courage.

Then the escalator reached the top, and Lorna stumbled off, still not sure she'd heard correctly. Nick caught her in time, and they both began to laugh.

"What the hell's going on?" Washington demanded, arriving just a step behind them. "Don't make a scene. You'll blow it before we get started."

Sobered but still elated, they joined hands and approached the ballroom. The reception was guarded by a table of beautifully dressed women who were checking invitations against a master list. Nick presented two engraved vellum cards from inside his dinner jacket and presented them with a smile. Behind them, Washington pretended he didn't know them. For his trouble, he got a disapproving look for wearing a suit, not formal clothes.

Then Nick and Lorna entered the ballroom hand in hand.

For a while, they circulated the room, saying nothing to each other, only touching. They drank champagne and enjoyed the spectacle—Dallas Cowboy cheerleaders were the center of attention, with a choir of children singing in another corner for the added pleasure of the high-paying donors. A photographer came out of nowhere and snapped their picture together, then asked for their names.

"For our 'About Town' column," he said, handing Nick a card. "You know. *The Bulletin*. Can I have your names, in case we use this photo?"

"Tom, you idiot. It's me!" Nick was exasperated. "Don't you recognize me?"

The photographer blinked and stared. "Nick? No kidding, is that you? What *happened?* You look great!"

"Everyone's a critic," Nick muttered, guiding Lorna away.

The party was going strong, with perhaps three hundred people milling around the large room. Lorna had never seen so many men wearing evening clothes and Stetson hats. Everyone took time to stroll past an easel that held a large poster upon which were written the names of people who had contributed to the charity. Lorna looked carefully and saw Martin Angelino's name inscribed at the top.

Time was running out, she knew. The reception was due to end in less than an hour, and it was impossible to guess if Angelino intended to stay until the end or leave early. Lorna noted that many people were already easing for the doors.

One young woman who was wearing an abbreviated cowboy costume, complete with toy six-guns, walked by carrying a handful of tickets for a charity draw. On impulse, Lorna caught her arm. "Excuse me, but may I borrow one of your guns for a minute?"

The woman looked startled. "Why?"

"Oh, darlin'," Nick broke in, convincingly portraying a long-suffering Texas husband, "you're not gonna pull that ol' trick on your po' daddy again?"

"Just this one more time, honey?" Lorna wheedled. "May I have the gun?"

"Here," Nick said, and he reached for his pocket. "Let me buy some of your tickets, li'l lady."

The promise of a sale made the woman more willing to give up her gun, so Lorna took it quickly and patted Nick's arm, drawling, "I'll be right back, honey."

"Be careful, darlin'," Nick drawled.

It's now or never, Lorna thought. With the toy gun in her hand, she made a beeline for the dance floor, where she had seen Angelino just a few minutes earlier. She wound her way through the crowd, her heart suddenly beating very hard. The whole room felt like a tunnel suddenly—spinning off-kilter and sounding very loud.

Angelino was standing near the punch bowl, joshing with a tight bunch of other men. They laughed suddenly, throwing their heads back, as if someone had told a dirty joke.

Lorna went straight to him and pasted a smile on her face. "Aren't you Marty Angelino?"

He was about her height, but managed to look down the length of his haughty nose at Lorna. He smiled— sure of himself, but not sure of who she was, yet liking what he saw. "Yes. And you are?"

"We met a few years ago," Lorna said quickly. "How about dancing with me? For old time's sake?" She pointed the toy gun at him then, trembling and trying to keep the smile in place. "Come on, Marty."

He laughed at the joke and lifted his hands as if in a holdup, grinning around at the circle of his friends. "Sure. Anything you say, honey, just don't shoot me."

His friends chuckled.

On the dance floor, only half a dozen other couples were dancing. It hadn't occurred to Lorna that he would actually have to touch her until her feet hit the parquet floor. She stopped so suddenly that he collided with her from behind.

Lorna spun around and said breathlessly, "Let's just talk, instead."

"You sure?" He looked disappointed, but game for anything. He did a quick Latino-style dance step as if to coax her. "I'd like to see how you use that body, honey."

Lorna felt her smile turn icy. "Come over here."

A few steps away, they were standing in the partial privacy created by a large fig tree.

He said, "What did you say your name is?"

"You don't remember me, do you?"

"Should I?" He narrowed his eyes, but kept smiling, trying to place her. "Are you a friend of Linda's?"

"Nope. Just you."

He grinned. "Did we have a thing going?"

"What do you mean by 'a thing'?"

He waggled his eyebrows and took a step closer. "I know a lot of girls. But I think I'd remember you."

"My hair was different. Shorter."

"Okay, okay. Did you work at Mario's? Or did we just go to bed together?"

"There wasn't a bed," Lorna said flatly.

He caught the change in her voice, and smiled for real. "Oh, I get it. Hey, were you the one in the basement? The one on the floor of the super's office? Near the laundry."

"At Harborside Apartments, yes, that was me." Lorna felt herself shaking, but she couldn't stop. "You grabbed me around the neck and held me down on the floor until I passed out."

He began to laugh. "You shouldn't have fought me, honey. Yeah, I remember you. You bit me, right?"

"Only because you hit me first. I didn't want you to touch me at all. I told you no."

"Yeah, but you loved it in the end," he said, reaching out to finger the sleeve of her jacket. "You're back for more, aren't you? That's why you brought me over here, right?"

Lorna jerked back from his hand. "You're a rapist, Mr. Angelino."

"Oh, that's just a rumor started by some ugly women. I don't have to rape anybody. I'm a good-looking guy! I've got girls hanging all over me all the time."

"But you like to hurt women."

He shrugged. "Some people like it rough. It's exciting."

"Is it exciting to stalk women in your own building?"

He grinned, puzzled. "What is this, anyway?"

"I just wondered how you get your tenants."

With another laugh, throwing his head back again, he said, "Oh, I can pick 'em, can't I? The ones who need my kind of hospitality. The quiet ones like it best. They're the ones who don't bite me, you know."

"I'm glad I bit you."

But he didn't hear that. Almost bragging, he said, "I find 'em in shelters sometimes. I give 'em a home, and they're grateful. They don't bite," he added reproachfully.

"And you rape them?"

He shrugged. "I don't call it that."

"But you force them."

"Hey, it turns me on, you know?" He grinned. "And you really turn me on, too, honey. You could be hot."

It was purely instinct, Lorna decided later, that she chose that moment to point the toy gun at Angelino as he stepped close, backing her into the tree.

He saw the gun and hesitated. "Hey, that thing isn't real, is it?"

Lorna said, "What do you think?"

He laughed—not sounding as confident as he had a moment ago. "I think it's a fake. You're kidding me, right?"

Lorna could see Detective Washington coming toward her, his face set as he reached into his hip pocket and came up with the handcuffs. Before he made it to Angelino, though, Lorna lifted the gun and pointed it directly at the face of the man who had raped her two years ago.

The expression that came to his eyes at that moment—it was absolute mortal fear—sent a heady rush of victory sweeping through Lorna's body.

"Bang!" she said.

And Washington grabbed Angelino's wrist, whipping it behind his back with such force that the man cried out. "Martin Angelino," Washington said, "you are arrested for rape..."

Lorna didn't hear any more. The noise of the crowd suddenly turned into a roar like a tremendous waterfall in her ears, deafening her, confusing her. She felt very alone suddenly, as if the rest of the room had begun to recede like the ocean's undertow—sweeping out to sea in a great, uncontrollable suction.

But then Nick was there, murmuring in her ear, drawing her away from the noise and prying the toy out of her hand.

"Let go," he was saying. "Lorna, let me have the gun. It's over, love. It's over."

Her silence scared the hell out of Nick. So did her doll-like immobility. He helped the cops unfasten the tape that held the microphone to her body, wincing as her delicate skin was pulled by the adhesive. But Lorna barely noticed, not even as Nick rebuttoned her blouse.

"She did great," said one of the cops in the listening van. "There won't be any accusation of entrapment. I was nervous when he said something about a gun, though. What happened, Fortune? Did you see it?"

"It was a toy," Nick said, bundling Lorna out of the van. She had begun to shiver, despite the heat, and he wrapped her in his dinner jacket to prevent shock.

Washington had put his prisoner in a squad car, but he walked over to have a look at Lorna. He shook his head. "Take her home, Fortune."

"That's all you have to say? She did your job for you, pal."

"So what else is new?" Washington cracked. "Just take care of her, all right?"

Nick put Lorna into the front seat of the Mercedes he'd borrowed from Hal, his architect friend. When he'd gotten in beside her and started the car, she still didn't speak. That's when Nick decided something drastic was needed.

Ten

From Lorna's hotel room, Nick called *The Bulletin* and dictated the story of Angelino's arrest to a stenographer.

"Tell Hoolihan he can edit the piece any way he likes," Nick said. "And tell him I'm taking a vacation."

Then he helped Lorna pack a suitcase and took her to the old homestead—Lost Fortune, the place of his birth, the ranch that time forgot.

His family was astonished by the car, at first. Then by Lorna's wan beauty.

"You didn't steal that car, son," said his father, who had never quite trusted any of his notoriously mischievous children, "did you?"

"Pop, won't you ever trust me? I'm a grown man now, not a troublemaking kid," Nick teased his father.

Ralph Fortune gave him a withering look. "I may be getting old, but I'm not stupid, boy. How about this girlfriend? Where did she come from?"

"Back East," Nick replied, watching as his mother and sister Darla Jean ushered Lorna out of the heat and into the low-slung house. He was glad to see Lorna making an effort to converse with the other women. She had been eerily silent during their long drive.

"Who is she?" Ralph asked, dragging off his hat and dusting it against his jeans. He had just gotten off a horse and still held the reins, having probably put in two hours' worth of work before breakfast.

"She's a writer for the paper."

"That's all?" Ralph's squint was shrewd. "I wondered if she's the one responsible for you looking like some kind of penguin. Where'd you get that suit of clothes, anyhow?"

"I bought it," Nick said with a grin, opening his dinner jacket to reveal his immaculately starched shirt. He hadn't taken the time to change, just made straight for the ranch some time after midnight. "I'm almost respectable now."

"Almost," Ralph agreed dryly. "Still got that infernal earring, I see. Why a grown man sticks himself like some kind of savage—"

"I didn't do it myself."

"Another girlfriend," Ralph said with a short laugh. "Well, I hope this one has more sense than all the rest of them you've got stashed back in Dallas."

"I don't have any girlfriends stashed away anymore, Pop."

"Oh, yeah? What's that mean, exactly? This one's the last, huh?"

"Maybe so," Nick said with a grin.

"That's why you brought her out here? To show her to your mama?"

"That, too," Nick told him. "But she needs a rest, I think. She's had a tough time lately."

Ralph nodded sagely, understanding the stress of city living and the need to return to the land now and then. "She'll be okay here," he said. "Your mama needs somebody to fuss over."

Which was about as close to father-son intimacy that Nick could ever remember.

Without another word, Ralph lumbered off to see to his horse and said over his shoulder, "Don't let anybody eat my breakfast, you hear?"

A couple of days at Lost Fortune did bring the color back into Lorna's face. Nick took her riding every morning, and they went swimming at the creek at twilight every evening. In between, Lorna napped, read or helped the other women in the kitchen. One afternoon, she sat on the fence rail and watched Ralph work with a green colt, even taking her turn with the lunge line.

Nick tried to give her space. But as he got to know Lorna during those several days, his longing to get closer to her grew exponentially. He'd never known a woman he wanted to protect as much as he wanted to protect Lorna. Yet that was the one thing she seemed to want least from him.

She talked to Nick by the hour, though, but managed to avoid the one topic he knew she needed to get off her chest—the subject of Martin Angelino. She even left the room one morning when Nick took a call from Washington. She seemed determined to empty her mind of unpleasant events.

And she did not ask Nick into her bed at night.

He didn't pursue it, knowing that she'd reached a certain crisis within her own heart and needed time to settle it.

Darla Jean was blunt one evening when she brought an armload of clean laundry into Nick's room. She plunked the clean clothes on his bed and sat down beside them. "So, how come you're not sleeping together?"

"I beg your pardon?"

"Don't try joking your way around the subject, Nickie. This is your big sister talking. You and Lorna act like old lovers, but you're in this room and she's down the hall with her door shut. What's going on?"

"Maybe it's none of your business."

Darla Jean shook her head. "I'm the one who's been married three times, remember?"

How could anyone forget? Darla Jean had a habit of marrying a new rodeo rider every three years—always some poor, broke cowboy with a couple of nice horses but not a single dollar to rub between his fingers. True love just couldn't flourish in a financially barren relationship, so Darla Jean happened to be between husbands at the moment, which was why she was living under her parents' roof.

She continued in a drawl, "I can see there's something between you two, and I'm just itching to fix whatever it is. I'm such an old romantic. What is it?"

"Some bad history," Nick replied cautiously, hoping Darla Jean wouldn't clamp onto the subject like a bulldog.

"You did something rotten?"

"How come everybody assumes *I'm* the villain in this little soap opera? Hell, I'm the good guy!"

"Sorry." Darla Jean didn't look a bit sorry and relaxed into his pillows as if ready to stay for a long, long chat. "So why are you pussyfooting around? If you're the good guy, go for it!"

"She needs time."

Darla Jean shook her head. "In my opinion, time just makes wounds fester. You want some advice, little brother?"

"Do I have a choice?"

With a grin, Darla Jean said, "Make a move, Nickie. Do something before she decides you're nothing more than a nice guy."

"I *want* her to think I'm a nice guy!"

"Not too nice," Darla Jean advised, getting up from the bed and slouching out the door. "I'm going into town for a drink. You two want to tag along?"

"The rodeo's in town?" Nick guessed archly.

"Nope. It's a circus." Darla Jean grinned. "I thought I'd try a change of pace. How about you?"

Nick slipped a shirt over his head, thinking about his sister's advice. "I think I'll stay here. Have fun."

Darla Jean waved her fingertips and disappeared down the hall.

By the time Nick was finished dressing, he decided his sister was probably right.

Five minutes later he was tapping softly on Lorna's bedroom door.

Lorna sat at the desk and used a small hand mirror propped against a stack of old *National Geographic*s to wind her hair on top of her head in a bun. She heard a knock at her door and gave up trying to pin her hair.

"Yes?"

Nick opened the door and stuck his head in. "It's me. Darla Jean's leaving for a night on the town. You feel like going?"

Lorna hadn't bothered to dress again after their cool swim in the creek. She had put on her nightgown—a lacy, but modest thing—and sat at the desk getting ready for bed. She shook her head and stifled a lady-like yawn at the same time. "I'd fall asleep in the peanuts, I'm afraid."

"Good," Nick said, slipping into the room and closing the door behind himself. He looked very tall in the small room, and his hair was slicked back with water. Now that it was so short, however, his hair tended to stand up in spikes. It gave him a kind of punk-cowboy look that wasn't unattractive. "I didn't feel like going, either."

He sauntered into the room, looking around, bemused. It had been the bedroom of one of his younger brothers, apparently, for the walls had been decorated with a cowboy wallpaper. The curtains and bedspread had been sewn out of fabric that depicted bucking broncos and cactus. One large model airplane was still suspended from the ceiling, although the boy who had constructed it was long gone from the house—and flying his own plane in the far reaches of Alaska, according to Nick's mother. His room was still boyish and charming, though, and Lorna had felt quite comfortable in it.

Seeing Nick stretch his long frame out on the bed, however, gave Lorna a surprisingly uneasy feeling inside. When he gave a huge yawn, she said, "Tired?"

Nick lay on his belly and grinned. "All the fresh air goes straight to my head. But no, I'm not tired. Just relaxed, I guess. You?"

Lorna toyed with her hairbrush. "I feel relaxed, too. Thank you, Nick. For bringing me here. I guess I needed—well, some time to unwind."

He watched her from the bed, suddenly serious. "You were wound pretty tight, weren't you? Tighter than I first thought."

"I thought I'd spent two years getting over something," she admitted. "But actually, I think I was planning my..."

"Revenge?"

She shook her head. "That's not it exactly. I wanted some closure, I think. I wanted to know it was really over."

"It is over, Lorna."

With an odd smile, she said, "I know that now. Washington called with good news today, didn't he?"

"The indictment went smoothly. The judge asked for half a million in bail to make sure Angelino stays in jail until the trial. The prosecutors like all the evidence— including your preliminary deposition—and they don't foresee any hitches. To top off all that good news, Washington thinks he's getting a promotion, and he sends his thanks to you."

Lorna laughed. "I'm sure he said that only to get your goat."

Nick's answering grin was rueful.

"He likes you, Nick. Honestly, I think he does."

"I know that. He knows that. But we don't dare admit it." On a breath, Nick added, "It's a lot like what's going on with us."

Lorna set down her hairbrush. "Nick..."

"I'm listening."

She shook her head, not sure she could communicate all the complicated emotions that had begun to fill her during the past several days. "I'm sorry I dragged you into this."

"What do you mean? The story was mine—"

"That's not what I meant. The story was great. It's my problems I wish we could have avoided. I shouldn't have made you get involved."

"Did you see me kicking and screaming?"

"It's just— You've seemed so miserable since we got here."

"Miserable?"

Lorna shook her head. "I know I made you relive everything you went through with Tish. You didn't feel capable of supporting me."

"No, I didn't. At first."

She looked up at him. "What does that mean? Have you changed your mind about us?"

"I may be an unfeeling jerk most of the time, but I'm trying to change. I've tried to help you put the pieces back together this week—"

"And you've done a wonderful job." Lorna struggled to hold back a rush of tears that suddenly threatened to overwhelm her. He had been remarkably kind and patient all week, and Lorna was very grateful. And full of hope. "Oh, Nick, does this mean . . ."

Nick got up from the bed and began to pace. "Maybe this was the wrong way to start. Lots of things were against us. Can we go on together without remembering how we met and what brought us together?"

"I don't know."

"Me, neither. I like to think that we met over a story—a story like a lot of stories I've covered in my life."

"But this was different—"

"Yes. I got emotionally involved. And you came into my life." Nick halted and stood over her. "But that's what street reporting is, Cookie. One unpleasant subject after another, and they all drag me in. My job isn't weddings and garden parties."

"It's horrible sometimes. But you manage to put your own humanity into every story, Nick."

"I try." He bulldozed over her words, saying, "I know I can't change what happened to you, Cookie. I can't even make you forget it. But I can write about it. And I want to be around to make sure it doesn't happen again."

"Nick, love—"

"I want to take care of you—and don't give me any line about not needing anyone to do that, Cookie."

"I thought you couldn't handle it. I thought you didn't want any part of my problems."

"I've changed my mind." He reached out and caressed her hair. "We all need somebody to take care of us. I want to be the one for you."

"Do you need somebody, Nick?"

He came up with a grin. "Sure. Look what you've done for me already."

She managed a shaky smile, too. "I haven't done a thing except take you away from your job. We've been here for days. Hoolihan must be furious with you."

Nick shook his head. "He knew I needed a break. I was burned-out before you came to town. I can admit it now." A ghost of a smile crossed his face. "But you got me going again, Cookie. I'm back, thanks to you."

"I can't take credit."

He knelt by her chair then, gathering Lorna into his arms. "I felt dead, truly, I did. Tish's trouble, the lawsuit against the paper—it almost crushed me. My work wasn't making a difference anymore. But you—you made me see my job through your eyes, Cookie. And it is important. I'm doing good stuff, and I'm going to keep on doing it.''

Lorna smiled, trembling. ''You're my hero, Nick.''

He laughed. ''Do you mean that?''

It felt so wonderfully good to be in his arms again. Lorna melted against him instinctively. ''Yes, I mean it.'' The next words popped out before Lorna thought about them. ''And I love you.''

Nick's voice turned husky, ''I was afraid I'd never hear those words from you. I thought I'd missed my chance.''

''I love you, Nick Fortune.''

He kissed her forehead then, careful as a schoolboy. Then he brushed her lips softly—twice—and finally kissed her, long and gently. Lorna's heart contracted with emotion.

The kiss soon flared into something hotter, though, and Lorna wound her arms high around his neck, drawing Nick snugly against her nearly naked body to relish every nuance. He slid his fingers up into her hair and murmured something tender against her lips.

How have I stumbled upon such a man? Lorna's mind reeled as Nick gathered her up and dropped her gently onto the bed. *He's so right for me.*

On the bed, he nuzzled her throat, loosening her nightgown at the same time. ''Let me show you,'' he murmured, ''how much I love you.''

''Oh, Nick,'' she whispered as he drew the lacy wisp of garment off her body. His right hand slid swiftly to the quivering flesh of her inner thigh. ''I've missed you.''

''I've been right here.''

"Yes, and I love you for your patience," Lorna smiled tremulously up at him. "But here in my bed— this is where I've missed you most."

"I've wanted you—more than you can guess."

"I can guess," she whispered. "Those long evening swims in the creek?"

He laughed. "You guessed my real purpose?"

"The water was so cold! It had to be the equivalent of a cold shower."

"I noticed you swimming right beside me."

Lorna traced his smile with her finger. "I love watching your body, Mr. Fortune. A couple of times, I almost—well—"

"You weren't ready."

"But now—" Lorna began tugging his shirt up out of his jeans. Her head was swimming with desire. Just his closeness, his teasing hand lying ready on her thigh, made Lorna hungry for more. "Nick, make love with me."

"My pleasure," he whispered.

She undressed him with hands that shook with passion. Then Nick threw back the bedclothes and they were tumbling into the sheets together. Lorna wanted to touch him everywhere, and her tentative fingers soon had Nick alternately laughing and groaning with frustration. She followed each caress with her lips, savoring the quickness of his response, the heat of his golden skin. She kissed him, rubbed her nose in the crisp hair of his chest, inhaling his scent, breathing him in, kissing him. She wanted to swallow the very essence of the man, to make him hers forever.

His breath caught time and again, and he gasped once, grasping her hair hard and writhing with the pent-up tension. "Lorna— This won't last much longer if you don't stop..."

Tantalizing, she continued to excite him—building slowly from a gentle tease to the moment when Nick arched powerfully against her, barely holding back his own climax. She released him then, murmuring soothing love words, coaxing the return of his sanity.

Nick growled and flipped Lorna onto her belly. He pinned her to the bed and with sure hands began to massage her body. Firmly, he kneaded her back, gradually moving lower until Lorna gasped with each increasingly intimate touch. With her heart pounding, she felt him explore—his fingertips seeking the spots that brought her the most pleasure, teasing her senses, finally insinuating them inside her. He evoked a moan of pleasure from her throat with each small, exquisite thrust. Lorna put her face into the pillow and felt she might drown in the hazy fog that enveloped her. His breath was warm on her back, his hands deft and wonderful.

"Please!" she cried out at last. "I can't wait, Nick."

He flipped Lorna onto her back then, and she parted her thighs to settle Nick into the cradle of her body. A moment later, he was snugly pressing inside her, pinning Lorna to the bed with his own body. He went deep within her, murmuring, "Oh, yes, love."

Locked with him and shuddering with passion, Lorna ran her palms over his shoulders, his back. She loved the contours of his body—the lacing of muscle and sinew on strong bone. When she wrapped her legs around his hips, she could feel the tightness of his legs. He was wonderfully strong, and the fire that radiated from Nick sparked the same warm flame inside Lorna, too. Her heart smoldered most of all.

With the Texas wind whispering in the eaves, Lorna gave herself to Nick that night, body and soul. She felt loved and adored. She felt sexually vital and surrendered to the swift turbulence of her senses, exploding with starry passion as Nick propelled them over the brink of a starry ecstasy.

Later, murmuring in the dark, she told him again and again how much she loved him.

In the morning, Lorna felt deliciously tired, perfectly satisfied...and ready to return to Dallas and *The Bulletin*.

"I've got to get Hal's car back to him, too," Nick said as they lingered in the bedroom, dressing each other between long, welcoming kisses. "I'm sure he's not happy about getting my truck fixed and having to use it while I'm here."

"I think the truck's got character," Lorna told him. "I love it."

"But it's not exactly the right vehicle for a family man," he said with a devilish gleam in his eye. "I think I'll look around for something else."

Lorna said her farewells to Nick's family, and she was truly sorry to say goodbye. They had all been so helpful when she needed kindness most. His mother—a gentle woman with a quick sense of humor—gave Lorna some muffins and asked her to see that Nick ate a square meal at least once a day. Then she gave Lorna a heartfelt hug.

Back at *The Bulletin*, Nick was greeted like a long-lost warrior who had conquered distant lands. Upon his arrival in the newsroom, his colleagues swarmed around, congratulatory about the Angelino story and an award that was sure to come his way. There were lots of hoots over his haircut, too.

Some people gave Lorna credit for Nick's transformation. But it was clear they now knew about Lorna's connection to the Angelino story, and they weren't sure how to approach one of the man's victims. Shyly, most of them avoided her.

Except Nick's friend Cassandra, the sportswriter, who pumped Lorna's hand in the middle of the crowded newsroom. "Great story, kiddo," she said. "You gonna stick around with us now?"

"I'm not sure," Lorna said softly. "That depends on a lot of things."

Cassandra grinned. "Has he proposed yet?"

Lorna couldn't stop a smile of her own. "Why do you want to know?"

"I started an office pool, of course," Cassandra confided. "Everybody's put money in the pot. Some of us put money on Nick remaining a bachelor forever. And some of us are betting he'll ask you to marry him any minute."

"Which side are you on?"

Cassandra winked. "The right side. You gonna give me some inside information?"

"I'm not sure what to tell you," Lorna said. "The future depends on a lot of things."

"Maybe I can settle one of them," Frank said. He had come out of his office to join the commotion, but he looked as solemn as ever as he crooked a finger at Lorna. "Would you step inside with me, Miss Kincaid?"

Lorna left the impromptu party and entered Frank's office. He closed the door behind them and sat down at his desk.

Getting to the point was not one of Frank's faults. Gruffly, he said, "You're a good writer, Miss Kincaid. I'd like to offer you a job."

Lorna slowly sat down in the chair across the desk from him, and she smiled. "Is that you talking, Mr. Hoolihan, or my Uncle J.B.?"

Frank reached for a plastic cup half filled with coffee that stood on his desk. "Of course, J.B. owns this newspaper, but I have complete say-so concerning my staff—"

"But he asked you to hire me, didn't he?"

Frank looked uncomfortable and took a slug of coffee to cover it. "Maybe so. But you're a decent reporter, too, Miss Kincaid."

"Decent isn't great," Lorna interrupted.

"You have potential."

"You're hip-deep in potential, Mr. Hoolihan. I know how many excellent writers you have here." Lorna steeled herself to tell the truth. "Look, I know all about nepotism. I've been given jobs all my life by my uncle, and I appreciate the chances he's given me. But I hate proving myself, I can never completely assure everyone that I'm the real McCoy, not just the boss's niece. I don't want that here."

She had Frank's complete attention by then. He asked, "What *do* you want?"

Lorna shook her head, saying, "I thought I wanted to be a hard-news reporter. I thought I wanted to write the tough stories and make a difference in the world. But..."

"Yes?"

"I'm not cut out for it."

Looking grave, Frank said, "Your contribution to the Angelino story was first-rate."

"It hurt, though," Lorna said. "It hurt too much."

"You were involved," Frank reminded gently. "If I'd known how much you were involved, I'd never have let you take on the story. It won't be like that every time."

"I appreciate your kindness," Lorna said, speaking from the heart. "But I know where I belong now. I wanted to try street reporting, and I did. My roots are elsewhere."

"I think you could be good, Miss Kincaid."

"Thanks." She smiled. "Your opinion means a lot. And I know you wouldn't let my uncle muscle you into hiring me if you didn't think I could really do the job. But I can't take it."

"J.B.'s going to be unhappy." Frank sat back and looked none too delighted at the prospect of reporting her response to the newspaper's owner.

Lorna almost laughed. "Let me call him."

Frank gratefully pushed the telephone across the desk to Lorna. She knew the number by heart and quickly dialed her uncle's private office.

Ten minutes later, Nick knocked on the window of Frank's office. He opened the door without permission and stuck his head in. "What's going on? Frank, you're not trying to seduce this pretty lady, are you?"

"And risk a punch from you?" Frank leaned back in his chair. "I heard about the fight at Frannie's, you know. I had to pay the damages."

"It wasn't a fight," Nick corrected, strolling into the office. "And there were no damages. What's going on?"

"I just offered Miss Kincaid a job here at *The Bulletin.*

Excitement lit up Nick's dark eyes. "Great!"

"But she turned me down."

"What?" Nick swung on Lorna. "You turned him down?"

Lorna nodded. "I can't take the job, Nick."

"Why the hell not?"

"I'm not cut out for street reporting. You knew it all along."

"But you were terrific!"

"At a great cost," Lorna admitted. "I can't do it day in and day out. It would kill me, Nick."

Frank stood up. "I think I'll get some fresh coffee. You two kids have some things to discuss."

When they were alone, Nick carefully took Lorna by her shoulders. "Cookie, I know you had a rough time last week. But you made it. Just think about working here, working with me. Together we could—"

"We could do a lot of things, Nick," Lorna intervened, placing her hands on his chest to hold him back. "But we can't work together."

He looked dark and thunderous. "Then you're leaving? After everything we've—"

"Cool your six-guns," Lorna ordered, laughing. "Who said anything about leaving?"

"Lorna—"

"My uncle offered me a job—the job he really wants me to take. It's my aunt's column for the New York paper."

Nick's hands tightened, and his face was suddenly taut with anguish. "New York!"

"It's right for me, Nick." Lorna knew she was speaking the truth. "I've been groomed all my life to write fluff. And there's nothing wrong with it, either. Maybe it's not hard news, but it makes the world go 'round."

"Lorna—"

"I had my chance, Nick. And I liked it. But I think I had something to prove. Now that I've proven it, I'm ready to take the job that was meant for me."

"But New York," Nick said again.

Lorna touched his cheek. "Wait. I've pitched an idea to Uncle J.B. He's going to think about it. I could do a syndicated column that would appeal to all of the papers my uncle owns—not just fluff, but a commentary."

Nick hesitated, obviously liking the idea. "Syndication's nice work, if you can get it."

"I think I *can* get it," Lorna said. "And I could live anywhere in the country to do it."

Hope began to dawn in Nick's expression. "Even Texas?"

"At this point," Lorna said, "wild horses couldn't drag me out of Texas."

"Oh, love," Nick said, swooping down for a long and hungry kiss. "Marry me," he said between breathless kisses on her lips and face. "Marry me, Cookie."

"I love you, Nick. I want to be with you forever."

That was answer enough. Nick gathered Lorna into his arms and proceeded to kiss the stuffing out of her.

And outside the glass windows of Frank's office, cheers erupted—from the winners of the office pool.

*   *   *   *   *

**Relive the romance...
Harlequin and Silhouette
are proud to present**

A program of collections of three complete novels by the most requested
authors with the most requested themes. Be sure to look for one volume each
month with three complete novels by top name authors.

In January: **WESTERN LOVING**   Susan Fox
                                          JoAnn Ross
                                          Barbara Kaye

Loving a cowboy is easy—taming him isn't!

In February: **LOVER, COME BACK!**   Diana Palmer
                                          Lisa Jackson
                                          Patricia Gardner Evans

It was over so long ago—yet now they're calling, "Lover, Come Back!"

In March: **TEMPERATURE RISING**   JoAnn Ross
                                          Tess Gerritsen
                                          Jacqueline Diamond

Falling in love—just what the doctor ordered!

Available at your favorite retail outlet.

REQ-G

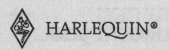

**Silhouette Books
is proud to present
our best authors,
their best books...
and the best in
your reading pleasure!**

Throughout 1993, look for exciting
books by these top names in
contemporary romance:

DIANA PALMER—
The Australian in October

FERN MICHAELS—
Sea Gypsy in October

ELIZABETH LOWELL—
Chain Lightning in November

CATHERINE COULTER—
The Aristocrat in December

JOAN HOHL—
Texas Gold in December

LINDA HOWARD—
Tears of the Renegade in January '94

When it comes to passion,
we wrote the book.   BOBT3

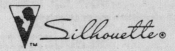

Christmas Classics

Share in the joys of finding happiness and exchanging the
ultimate gift—love—in full-length classic holiday
treasures by two bestselling authors

JOAN HOHL
EMILIE RICHARDS

Available in December at
your favorite retail outlet.

Only from 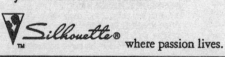 where passion lives.

SILHOUETTE.... Where Passion Lives

Don't miss these Silhouette favorites by some of our most popular authors!
And now, you can receive a discount by ordering two or more titles!

Silhouette Desire®

#05751	THE MAN WITH THE MIDNIGHT EYES BJ James	$2.89	☐
#05763	THE COWBOY Cait London	$2.89	☐
#05774	TENNESSEE WALTZ Jackie Merritt	$2.89	☐
#05779	THE RANCHER AND THE RUNAWAY BRIDE Joan Johnston	$2.89	☐

Silhouette Intimate Moments®

#07417	WOLF AND THE ANGEL Kathleen Creighton	$3.29	☐
#07480	DIAMOND WILLOW Kathleen Eagle	$3.39	☐
#07486	MEMORIES OF LAURA Marilyn Pappano	$3.39	☐
#07493	QUINN EISLEY'S WAR Patricia Gardner Evans	$3.39	☐

Silhouette Shadows®

#27003	STRANGER IN THE MIST Lee Karr	$3.50	☐
#27007	FLASHBACK Terri Herrington	$3.50	☐
#27009	BREAK THE NIGHT Anne Stuart	$3.50	☐
#27012	DARK ENCHANTMENT Jane Toombs	$3.50	☐

Silhouette Special Edition®

#09754	THERE AND NOW Linda Lael Miller	$3.39	☐
#09770	FATHER: UNKNOWN Andrea Edwards	$3.39	☐
#09791	THE CAT THAT LIVED ON PARK AVENUE Tracy Sinclair	$3.39	☐
#09811	HE'S THE RICH BOY Lisa Jackson	$3.39	☐

Silhouette Romance®

#08893	LETTERS FROM HOME Toni Collins	$2.69	☐
#08915	NEW YEAR'S BABY Stella Bagwell	$2.69	☐
#08927	THE PURSUIT OF HAPPINESS Anne Peters	$2.69	☐
#08952	INSTANT FATHER Lucy Gordon	$2.75	☐

AMOUNT	$ _____
DEDUCT: **10% DISCOUNT FOR 2+ BOOKS**	$ _____
POSTAGE & HANDLING	$ _____
($1.00 for one book, 50¢ for each additional)	
APPLICABLE TAXES*	$ _____
TOTAL PAYABLE	$ _____
(check or money order—please do not send cash)	

To order, complete this form and send it, along with a check or money order for the total above, payable to Silhouette Books, to: *In the U.S.*: 3010 Walden Avenue, P.O. Box 9077, Buffalo, NY 14269-9077; *In Canada*: P.O. Box 636, Fort Erie, Ontario, L2A 5X3.

Name: _____

Address: _____ City: _____

State/Prov.: _____ Zip/Postal Code: _____

*New York residents remit applicable sales taxes.
Canadian residents remit applicable GST and provincial taxes.

SBACK-OD